THE UNLEASHED SERIES

A MASTER'S *Destiny*

Red Phoenix

A Master's Destiny:
An Unleashed Series Standalone

Cover by Shanoff Designs
Formatted by BB eBooks
Phoenix symbol by Nicole Delfs

Dedication

Writing about Thane's experiences at the Dominant
Training Center is something I have longed to do
for years!

This one feels like traveling back in time to the first time
I wrote about Brie's experiences at the Submissive
Training Center–but from a completely new perspective.

I cannot tell you the fun I had writing it.

I loved getting to dive into who Master Nosh is as the
Head Trainer of the Dominant course. It was also fun to
meet the other trainers on the panel.

Starting with Thane on the first day of class was such a
treat, especially when we compare it to Brie's experiences
during her submissive training.

I must give my editor, KH Koehler, huge thanks for
helping to get this book out on time when it got down to
the wire and the story just wouldn't stop. She truly
worked tirelessly with little sleep!

Thanks also to Brenda, Becki and Marilyn, my awesome
proofers who took on the challenge.

As always, all my love to MrRed who not only loves and
supports me, but inspires the joyous fun found within
the pages.

To Jon and Ben who worked with heart and vision to
promote this book. Working with you is my joy.

To my incredible muses who always surprise and delight
me as I write. You have been faithful to this little author

from day one.
And of course to you, my dear readers. Your presence in
my life and your love and support of my work spurs me
on to keep writing every day.
Muah!

SIGN UP FOR MY NEWSLETTER
HERE FOR THE LATEST RED
PHOENIX UPDATES

FOLLOW ME ON INSTAGRAM
INSTAGRAM.COM/REDPHOENIXAUTHOR

SALES, GIVEAWAYS, NEW
RELEASES, PREORDER LINKS, AND
MORE!

SIGN UP HERE
REDPHOENIXAUTHOR.COM/NEWSLETTER-
SIGNUP

CONTENTS

Power Exchange 1

First Day of Training 2

Erotic Spanking 11

The Challenge 20

Lessons in Leadership 30

Electrify Me 41

Friends 50

Chastity 57

Perspective 68

Buddy 81

Three-way Tie 94

Honey 109

Compassion 123

Trust 134

Breathless 148

Suspicion 156

Treachery 168

Fiery Fun 181

Sparks 192

Ren Nosaka 202

Tainted Love	211
Power of Will	222
The Art of Flogging	231
Graduation Day	241
The Calling	253
Coming Next	268
About the Author	269
Other Red Phoenix Books	272

Power Exchange

(Beautiful Representation)

In the D/s dynamic, the Dominant's title is capitalized and the submissive's pet name is not.

It speaks to the power exchange between them and is a meaningful representation of the relationship in written form.

First Day of Training

Is it possible to fail as a Dominant?

When I pull into the parking lot at the Training Center, I feel a prickling sensation crawl across my scalp as that thought takes over. My nerves suddenly kick in as I turn off my car and stare blankly at the brick building.

My fear surprises me. Unlike many of the trainees attending the class tonight, I'm not new to the world of BDSM.

No, a few years ago when I was in college, my Russian friend, Anton Durov, opened my eyes to the life he led in secret. His introduction exposed me to a whole new world.

Although I have been enjoying BDSM clubs for several years now, I'm a perfectionist at heart. So, when I learned about the Dominant Training Center, I was eager to apply.

I know I still have a lot to learn as a Dominant, and what better way to improve my skills than to do so under the watchful gaze of experienced experts well versed in a variety of tools and techniques?

The opportunity to be mentored by four highly respected Dominants will put me lightyears ahead of where I would be on my own, and it's something I can't pass up.

However, the course isn't cheap, and it will require all of my free time outside of work if I am to succeed in the coming six weeks.

The instructors here have warned me that this course will test my strength and resolve as a Dominant, but I am ready to meet the challenge, which is why my current state of unease comes as a shock to me.

Rather than allow doubts to derail me, I force myself out of the car and straighten my suit jacket.

A pompous-looking guy with a golden tan and long blond hair gives me a condescending look as he strolls past. His shirt is unbuttoned, showing off his muscular chest. He looks as if he's just come from the beach after a day of surfing. Glancing at my car, he sneers, "Nice wheels."

I gaze affectionately at the old sedan my uncle gave me as a graduation gift after college. Although the silver car is covered in scratches and small dents from years of use, she has never failed to get me where I need to go. Unashamed of the car I've nicknamed Motivation, I give her a loving pat, and murmur, "Don't listen to the prick."

I look up and watch the guy head to the entrance, walking with a cocky swagger as if he owns the place.

Shaking my head, I chuckle to myself. *I'd love to see where we are ten years from now…*

I have big plans for my future.

Straightening the collar of my suit, I head toward the unassuming brick building that houses both a business college and the world-renowned Training Center on its lower level. No one passing by this college would ever suspect the kinky curriculum being taught inside its walls.

My nervousness starts to abate the moment I stop to open the entrance door for the young woman with strawberry blonde hair walking behind me.

She looks me up and down with a flirtatious smile and murmurs, "Nice suit," as she passes by me.

I nod in response, intrigued by the spark of chemistry between us. I continue to watch her as she makes her way through the large foyer and heads to a hall lined with business classrooms. She turns her head and glances back at me coyly before disappearing into the crowd.

Glancing down at my watch, I head directly to the reception desk. Rachael, a staple of the Training Center, bows her head slightly as I approach. "Good evening, Mr. Davis."

She knows me because I've come several times as an observer to watch classes at the Submissive Training Center at the invitation of Marquis Gray, who happens to be a trainer here.

"It's a pleasure to see you again, Miss Dunningham," I reply casually, even though the nerves have started up again. This is the first time I've come as a student of the school, and it feels distinctly different.

Rachael responds with an engaging smile. "You'll want to take the elevator down and go to the hallway to your right. You'll find your classroom at the end of that hall." Her smile widens when she adds, "Enjoy your first class, Mr. Davis."

I nod in thanks and start toward the elevator. I'm here tonight because I was personally invited to join this session of the Dominant Training Class. I understand how fortunate I am, considering the waiting list for applicants is already a year out.

I remind myself of that as I step into the elevator. I feel more confident about the night ahead and am determined to meet whatever challenges the trainers throw at me. But, just as the doors begin to shut, I hear a familiar voice command, "Hold the doors."

I immediately reach out to stop the elevator doors from closing and watch as Marquis Gray enters. He gazes at me with those dark, penetrating eyes before nodding curtly. "Sir Davis."

I clear my throat, and respond in a formal tone, "Marquis Gray."

The man is tall but has a thin build and unusually pale skin. Marquis Gray has a powerful aura that commands respect whether you personally know him or not.

He is well respected in the BDSM community for his talent and skill. However, he is best known for his uncanny ability to see straight into a person's soul with those dark eyes. Besides being a pillar in the community, he is also one of the trainers at the exclusive Submissive Training Center.

Ever since it opened its doors a little over ten years ago, the Center has become world-renowned for its unique program and the exceptional quality of its submissives. To this day, the Center has continued to produce top-notch students.

It was due to the Submissive Training Center's un-precedented success that they were recently able to launch the Dominant Training course. I owe Marquis Gray because he was the one who personally invited me to join this session.

I hope to prove his confidence in me is justified.

"Are you prepared for this evening?" Marquis asks, staring straight ahead as the elevator heads down.

"I believe so."

He nods without turning his head, but I catch the slight smirk on his lips. I get the feeling Marquis Gray doesn't think I am.

When he steps out of the elevator, I hear him say quietly, "Follow your instincts."

Before I can respond, Marquis Gray takes an abrupt left and heads toward the Submissive wing of the building.

I scan the large commons area briefly and take a deep breath, mulling over his words. Then I turn in the opposite direction as Marquis Gray and head to the Dominant wing of the school.

My excitement builds with each step I take. I know this Dominant training course is going to change my life. I can feel it in my bones.

Walking into the classroom, I'm startled to see the same pompous guy who'd insulted my car in the parking lot. I take a seat on the opposite side of the classroom and glance up at the clock, surprised to see the instructor isn't here yet.

I casually glance at the other students, curious about the people I'll be working with for the next six weeks.

Besides the Surfer Boy, there are only five other men and two women. I happen to catch the eye of a woman sitting next to me. I feel her eyes studying me as if she's making an assessment.

She looks older than I am, possibly in her thirties. Based on her facial features and the dark brown curls cascading down her back, I suspect she's of Hawaiian descent. She's so striking and elegant, that I wonder if she might be a model.

"Hey, sexy," the man sitting on the other side of her pipes up. He has an overly polished look with his hair slicked back and several gold rings on his fingers.

The woman turns in her chair and stares at him but says nothing.

He leans in closer. "Are you a lesbo?"

I hear the disdain in her voice when she responds. "What did you just say?"

"I hear most Dommes are lesbians, but I don't have a problem with that." He raises his eyebrows suggestively, telling her, "I bet it's hot when you go down on another chick."

I glare at him, offended by his words, and bark, "Apologize to her at once."

The woman raises her hand to me. "Thank you, but I can handle this."

I nod to her and bite back my anger, but my blood is

boiling.

The guy looks at me smugly, then whispers to her, "Have you tried cock? I'd be happy to introduce you to mine. I've had no complaints…"

I grit my teeth, desperate to punch the man.

The woman lifts her chin higher as she faces forward and stares at the whiteboard in silence, a slight smile on her lips. When the bell finally rings for the class to begin, she stands up and walks up to the teacher's desk.

I chuckle to myself, suddenly realizing who she is.

Turning to face the class, she begins, "I will be your instructor for the next six weeks. You shall address me by my last name, which is Alana."

She scans the classroom, making eye contact with each student as she continues, "As a student of this course, you represent the Training Center at all times, whether you are in class or out in the vanilla world."

Alana's gaze lands on the insolent man, and he shifts uncomfortably in his chair. In a cool voice, she states, "Being a Dominant is about respect. Respect for yourself *and* for others. At the Center, we will not tolerate offensive or abusive behavior. If we hear of any of our students behaving in such a way, they will be immediately cut from the program."

She picks a piece of paper off the table and briefly glances at it before reading off the name of the man who insulted her. "Mr. Walker…" She looks him straight in the eyes when she tells him, "You have been cut from the program."

"You can't do that!" he snarls, banging his fist on his desk. "I spent good money on this course."

"Your money will be refunded. The Center has no interest in training you."

"It was just harmless flirting." He laughs, looking around at the other students for validation. "People do it all the time, right?"

"Mr. Walker, please leave."

Walker refuses to budge from his chair, stating begrudgingly, "You made your point."

"You don't seem to understand. I'm not asking you to leave, I'm telling you."

He stares at Alana in shock, but eventually, he gets up and starts walking to the door. Looking back at the other students in the room, he grumbles, "I can't believe I'm getting kicked out of the program by a dyke."

Alana picks up the phone at her desk. "Mrs. Dunningham, please see that Mr. Walker is escorted out of the building."

After hanging up the receiver, she faces us again, her demeanor calm and authoritative. "I have found over the years that sitting in on the first day of class provides me with vital information."

I notice several of the other students glancing at each other nervously, seemingly concerned by the impression they've unwittingly made with their instructor. I chuckled to myself, wondering how many of them attempted to hit on her before class.

"Do you have something to say, Mr. Davis?" Alana asks me.

I meet her gaze, feeling nothing but respect for our instructor. "I'm impressed with how you handled the situation."

She nods curtly before addressing the entire class. "We will begin by discussing the cornerstone behind every BDSM encounter—clear and concise communication. Listen carefully, because your first practicum will be directly tied to this lecture."

Knowing that I will be scening with a submissive after this class definitely has my interest piqued…

Erotic Spanking

"**R**aise your hand if you are familiar with the term 'safeword'."

Only two of us in the class raise our hands. Ironically, it's me…and Surfer Boy.

Alana nods. "It's imperative as a Dominant that you establish safewords before you begin a scene with a new partner." She pauses for a moment to emphasize the importance of her statement and allow it to sink in.

"Some of the most common safewords used are the colors red, yellow, and green to indicate comfort level. However, you and your partner can establish any unusual word or action to stop a scene immediately. Think of it as a safety net. As a Dom, you can never predict how a scene will play out, and the last thing you want is to cause harm to your partner. An established safeword allows both parties to end a scene immediately without question."

"Why would a Dominant ever need one?" asks a distinguished man with a trimmed beard and tailored suit sitting in the back.

Alana turns to him. "Ask me that again *after* I have called on you."

He immediately apologizes before raising his hand.

"Yes, Mr. Ravenson. What was your question?"

Ravenson clears his throat, clearly embarrassed for speaking out of turn. "If a Dominant is in charge of playing out the scene they've created, why would they need a safeword?"

I agree with his question, having never used one myself, so I am interested in our instructor's answer.

"Excellent question," she compliments him. "There are several occasions when a Dominant might need to call out a safeword. One prime example would be if you found yourself questioning your sub's ability to call out their safeword during a scene. Or, if for whatever reason, you felt your sub needed to call it but couldn't or wouldn't, you might call it for them."

She pauses for a moment, stating, "Safety must always come first."

"Another example would be if you simply needed to take a break or stop altogether because you were not enjoying the scene."

One of the other men frowns and raises his hand.

"Yes, Mr. Lofton?"

"Does it really matter as long as your submissive is getting off on it?"

She smiles. "Of course it matters. Both partners should enjoy the scene they've agreed to play out together. Naturally, as a Dominant, you can choose to sacrifice your enjoyment in order to please your sub. However, that is a conscious choice you must make for yourself. Never forget that you are in control of the scenes you create, and there is no shame in stopping if you become uncomfortable."

Alana begins to slowly pace back and forth in front of the room. "Another thing to keep in mind is that playing the role of the Dominant can be physically taxing on the body. You may experience too much pain or fatigue to continue your scene."

Ravenson nods in understanding.

"But it's not just the physical aspect," she states in a somber tone. "There is also another—often over-looked—element to being a Dominant. You may have scenes that challenge you emotionally and may cause you internal conflict." She stops pacing and looks at us thoughtfully. "Never dismiss your emotions, and do not lose sight of the fact that you are responsible for *two* people's safety and well-being."

I appreciate Alana's advice. I know myself well. It would be easy for me to forget that in my desire to not disappoint the sub I'm scening with.

Alana continues, "Be aware that your submissive will be extra sensitive to your emotions during a scene. If you ever get the sense that the scene feels 'off' to you, your sub will immediately pick up on it. Should that happen, I suggest you call your safeword to stop it. Talk through it if you feel you can continue. Otherwise, end the scene and revisit it at a later date."

She faces us and states, "As a Dominant, there is no shame in calling your safeword. Let me repeat that in case you missed it. A Dom should feel no shame in refusing to play out a scene that makes them uncomfortable. We expect our submissives to be open and honest about their limits, and we must be equally honest with them—and ourselves."

Alana frowns. "It is easy to get caught up in the power that comes from giving our subs what they want. However, that power can steer a Dominant in a dangerous direction."

The entire class is riveted on her, every student responding to the somber tone of her voice.

"When you agree to a scene, you must not only be prepared mentally, but you *must* be qualified to use the tool or technique. It is an inexcusable breach of trust to scene unless you know exactly what you are doing."

She pauses for a moment. "Because, if you don't, it can lead to accidents or…even death."

I noticed the pained look in Alana's eyes when she tells us, "I lost a good friend that way. The Dominant she was scening with lied to her about his experience because he wanted to impress my friend. The man had no business performing predicament bondage." Her voice catches for a moment. "He ended up killing her during the scene in front of a live audience."

I groan, sickened by the thought. Without warning, a vision of my friend Durov tied to his bed, bloody and bruised, flashes in my head. In an instant, I am taken back to that night, and I relive the intense guilt I felt on seeing the damage Samantha caused as an inexperienced Domme. In her desire to impress him, Samantha caused Durov incredible pain. I have never been able to forgive myself and that night will always haunt me…

Alana turns to the whiteboard and writes the word *"Communication"* in capital letters.

She then explains that communication can take many forms, including a formal contract. "Normally, a contract is part of the fantasy, much like a prop. It can be erotic and sexy for both partners to sign a document entitling one partner to exclusive rights over another person's body and will.

"Although very few people who practice BDSM actually use one, a contract can act as a useful guide for documenting pertinent information for both partners. Think of it as a reference sheet for everyone involved. But it's important to note, a BDSM contract is *not* a legal document and cannot be used as evidence in a court of law."

Surfer Boy chuckles, catching her attention and she immediately asks, "What do you find so funny, Mr. Slater?"

A smirk plays across his face when he answers, "I'm just imagining some idiot going up to a judge and handing him the contract to prove his innocence. That joker would be laughed right out of the courtroom."

"Which is why it would be remiss of me not to mention it," she states dryly. "Unfortunately, there are predators who pose as Dominants, and they purposely misinform submissives, making them believe such a contract is legally binding and cannot be broken."

I shake my head, disgusted by the misuse of power.

"For most Dominants, formal contracts are unnecessary. However, it *is* vital that you know your partner's limits and any items that are deal breakers for them."

The lone female student in the class raises her hand.

"Yes, Miss Reid?"

"How exactly do you find that out?"

Alana smiles. "I'm glad you asked." Walking back to the whiteboard, she informs us, "There are certain things you should ask whenever you meet a potential partner for the first time."

"Here are some of the questions to ask." She writes the number one, then writes out her words as she speaks. *"What experience do you have as a submissive?"* She turns to face us. "This allows you to gauge the level of your sub's experience during your power exchange."

Writing the number two, she says, *"What characteristics do you find sexy in a Dominant, and what turns you off?"* She smiles at us. "Knowing what turns them off is often as enlightening as what turns them on."

Looking back at the whiteboard, she writes the number three. *"What kinds of scenes turn you on?"*

After writing the number four, she says, *"Tell me about some things that you haven't tried but would like to?"*

"And last, but one of the most important questions to ask," she states, underlining the question. *"Do you know your limits?"*

I look at the list of questions, appreciating how concise and informative they are.

After a lengthy discussion about the questions, Alana informs us that we will be leaving her classroom to head to our first practicum.

"The trainers have gone over your applications and have chosen a submissive based on your answers."

Lofton's hand shoots up again, his voice raising in

pitch when he asks, "Are we expected to scene with them?"

Alana's tone is soothing and calm when she explains, "Yes. This first practicum will involve a simple spanking scene."

We instantly turn to the door and watch as a young submissive enters the room. She is completely naked and bows to the instructor.

Alana nods to her in acknowledgment. "Lean against my desk with your shapely ass facing my students."

"Yes, Mistress Alana."

Alana runs her hand over the sub's bare skin, telling us, "I am going to give you several pointers on how to give an erotic spanking."

Once again, she captures the class's attention as she explains, "You want to begin with foreplay. Before a spanking session, you want to start by rubbing and caressing their buttocks to warm up the skin before you begin."

As she speaks, Alana demonstrates her actions, tenderly rubbing the submissive's heart-shaped ass.

"The way you hold your hand will determine how the slap feels. Keeping your fingers together will hurt less." She gives the sub a playful slap with just the palm of her hand, and the sound of it rings through the room.

"If you cup your hand, you will increase the depth of sound without affecting the pain level." She smacks the submissive again, producing a deeper slapping sound.

Alana then points to the area below the tailbone and down to the upper thighs. "Hit only the fleshy part of the butt and use an upwards motion like this." She begins swatting the submissive's ass lightly.

"Take a break between each swat or between combinations of swats so you can leave your submissive waiting in anticipation. You can graze your hand over your partner's skin, play with their genitals, or rub your palm on their cheeks in a circular motion." She demonstrates each motion as she says them. "You can even do nothing and let them guess when and where the next impact will be…"

Alana slaps her sub's ass harder in the same spot several times. The submissive yelps but then purrs when Alana stops. Instantly, the submissive's ass cheek begins to pinken. "Understand, that when you hit someone in the same spot repeatedly, you will create a bruise. If you continue hitting them while that bruise is forming, it can actually cause harm."

She tenderly rubs the area she just spanked before continuing, "To prevent that, make sure to cover the whole surface so that both buttocks are getting stimulated rather than focusing on just one spot over and over again."

The room fills with the erotic sound of her slapping. "Now, if your sub gets really turned on, but one area is getting increasingly red, you can move to another area and return to it later on."

Alana gives the submissive one more spirited slap before ending the lesson.

"Thank you, starlight."

It's obvious by the sparkle in the submissive's eyes that she has thoroughly enjoyed the short demonstration. "Thank you, Mistress Alana."

She bows again before leaving the room.

Turning back to Lofton, Alana informs him, "The trainers will not be evaluating your spanking technique tonight but, rather, how you apply everything I've shared today."

Her answer seems to please him, and he sighs in relief.

However, the sexual energy in the room is now palpable as each of us contemplates scening with a stranger. I have to admit the idea of it is quite…stimulating.

"Before you leave, I have something for each of you," she informs us.

I'm the first to walk up to her desk and am presented with a tool bag. It's a long black bag made of leather with a golden emblem on it. Studying the emblem more closely, I read the Latin words, *Regere*, *Honorare*, and *Dominari*—Guide, Honor, and Dominate—and realize I'm looking at the official crest of the Dominant Training Center.

"You are expected to bring your tool bag to class every day with the appropriate tools for each night's practicum."

With my official Dominant Training tool bag in hand, I leave the room ready to face my very first practicum.

The Challenge

As we head down the hallway, I glance at my six other classmates.

Slater, AKA Surfer Boy, struts down the hallway in the lead. I doubt he will make it far in this program due to his massive ego.

The bearded man Ravenson, who wasn't afraid to ask questions in class, walks beside me.

Looking to the left of him I see Miss Reid, a young woman with dark hair and a gothic style. She looks to be lost in her own thoughts.

Bringing up our rear, Lofton whispers to one of the other students in front of me and smacks the guy's shoulder numerous times, clearly excited about the spanking session ahead.

The last guy walks several paces behind our group. He is staring straight ahead with his arms crossed. He's got a crew cut and glasses. The man's solitary demeanor invites no interaction and that intrigues me. I wonder if he is a natural loner or if he is simply observing all of us in silence and is drawing his own conclusions.

When I enter the room, my eyes are instantly drawn to the long table where the four trainers are sitting. I know from my conversations with Marquis Gray that Master Nosh, who sits at the far left of the table, is the Head Trainer of this Dominant course. Due to his proud Cheyenne heritage and his extensive expertise as a Dom, he is a formidable presence in the room.

Beside him sits a bald man with a muscular physique. He stares at us like a drill sergeant evaluating his newest recruits.

Sitting next to him is a man who has brown hair and pale blue eyes. He has facial features that hint at a Spanish or Portuguese ancestry. He stares at us with a critical eye, and I already have the impression that I am lacking in some way.

But the last man sitting on the right is a striking contrast to the other three. He has a burly red beard and greets us with a relaxed smile as if he is meeting old friends.

We line up in front of the panel of trainers and wait in silence.

Master Nosh slowly stands to address us. "Tonight, we will see how well you utilize what Alana went over with you in class. To be clear, we are only interested in investing our valuable time in students who are not only willing but are also able to take direction."

I notice Lofton stiffen beside me.

"As you've already learned, we are quick to eliminate anyone who fails to live up to the high standards of this institution."

If anyone thought this class was going to be easy, Master Nosh just blew that notion clear out of the water. As I stand there, looking at the four distinguished trainers, I am humbled to have the opportunity to work with such talent.

The Head Trainer continues, "We looked over the applications you filled out, and we have selected submissives based on your answers." He gestures to a row of spanking benches set near a mirrored wall on the other side of the room. "You will be playing out a spanking scene, but what that looks like is between you and your submissive."

The sexual energy in the room amps up the minute we hear the sound of clicking heels coming down the hallway, announcing the arrival of our submissives.

I close my eyes for a moment and take a deep breath. Although I have scened at clubs before, I have never done so under the watchful eye of four experienced trainers.

I recall when my Russian friend Anton Durov shared that his father observed him the very first time he scened with a submissive. Hell, if he can survive that kind of pressure, I'm certain I can handle this.

I open my eyes and turn my head to watch as the submissives parade into the room with their eyes lowered. I note that there are six women and one man.

They line up before the panel and bow their heads to the trainers in respect.

When Master Nosh gives the command, they gracefully move to the person they've been assigned to scene with and bow at their feet.

I look down at a woman in pigtails with pink streaks in her hair. She's wearing a rainbow tutu and has unnaturally long pink eyelashes and an abundance of eyeshadow and blush. I find it ironic since I mentioned on my application that I don't care for overdone makeup.

Out of curiosity, I glance at the other submissives and notice a wide range of ages, body types, and distinctive fashions.

Looking back down at the submissive bowing at my feet, a sense of protectiveness suddenly hits me knowing that the trainers have placed her under my care.

"You may begin your scene," Master Nosh announces to the class as he picks up a notebook. I notice all of the trainers have notebooks in hand as they start walking the room.

Lofton immediately orders his submissive to join him at the spanking benches, while I hear another of the students command his submissive to strip.

I question their haste and flippancy and take a completely different approach. Placing my hand on her head, I command my submissive to stand and follow me.

Rocking on her heels, the woman stands up but keeps her eyes lowered as she follows me to the far side of the room. Now that we have a little more privacy, I put my finger under her chin and lift her head so our eyes meet.

"During the scene, what name would you like me to call you by?"

"Lollipop."

I smile when I hear her pet name. "How charming."

She grins. "Thank you."

I become momentarily distracted when I notice one of the trainers stopping a short distance from me. He starts scribbling in his notebook.

Wondering what he is writing, I have to force myself to return my attention to my submissive. "You will call me Sir for this scene."

She nods eagerly. "Yes, Sir."

Remembering the questions Alana listed on the whiteboard, I ask in a casual tone, "Tell me, how long have you been in the lifestyle?"

"Five years, Sir."

It's good to know I have an experienced submissive. Curious about her relationship status, I ask, "Have you ever been collared?"

She shakes her head playfully, making her pigtails bounce. "Haven't found the right Dom yet, but I'm always looking."

I smile at her attempt to flirt with me. "Is it safe to assume that in five years, you've enjoyed a spanking scene or two?"

From the other side of the room, I hear the loud smack of a palm slapping against flesh.

The sound of it seems to turn us both on.

"Yes, I have, Sir," she answers, biting her lip as she glances in the direction of the benches.

"Do you like it hard or soft?"

The girl blushes when she answers. "Which part, the spanking or the fucking?"

I chuckle. "Both."

"To be honest with you, I have a low tolerance for pain, Sir. However, I love a good, hard thrust."

I nod at her teasing banter, thoroughly enjoying it. "So, you *do* have limits when it comes to spanking?"

She gazes into my eyes and says in a serious tone, "I don't like handprints, Sir."

I now know not to hit her with too much force, and I follow up my question with another. "No handprints," I agree, "but a pinkened ass is okay?"

"Not quite as pink as my hair," she replies, playfully twirling a strand of it with her fingers.

"A lighter shade of pink turns you on?"

She nods vigorously.

"And you'd like to end the session with hard penetration?" I growl hungrily.

Her eyes light up. "Yes, if it pleases you, Sir!"

Deciding I now have a good handle on her needs, I place my hand on her lower back and guide her to an empty spanking bench. Patting the leather padding on the wooden bench, I command, "Take off your panties and mount my bench."

She bites her bottom lip, squeaking in excitement. I watch her shimmy out of her pink panties and climb onto the bench. After she's settled, I take off my jacket and slowly roll up my sleeves.

"Do you enjoy restraints?" I play with one of the cuffs secured to the bench.

"I do, Sir."

With permission given, I bind her wrists first. I then trail my hand lightly over her back as I move to her legs. Once both of her ankles are bound in cuffs, leaving her completely helpless, I lift up her rainbow tutu to expose her naked ass.

Rubbing both buttocks tenderly, I remind her, "I want you to call out your safeword if I spank you too hard."

She turns her head to look at me. "What safeword would you like me to use, Sir?"

I grin, patting her butt lustfully. "Red, of course."

"Yes, Sir." She giggles, wiggling her ass to the alluring symphony of multiple submissives being spanked all around us.

I raise my hand and wait a couple of seconds before giving her a light swat. She giggles in response and begs, "Harder, Sir."

I begin by rubbing the area I plan to spank before giving her a playful slap. I continue spanking her in this way, switching between both butt cheeks, as I slowly increase the power of my hand.

I enjoy watching the way her fleshy ass ripples with each swat, while her skin begins to pinken.

All is going well until a submissive suddenly cries out, "Red!"

I turn in concern to see the loner in the hall now staring at his submissive in shock. One of his hands is still entwined in her long, blonde curls, while the other is poised to spank her again.

The room suddenly becomes deathly silent.

The guy slowly lowers both hands and steps back from her, looking confused.

"Mr. Ashford, why did your submissive call her safeword?" the bald trainer asks.

Ashford shakes his head when he answers. "I have no idea."

The trainer frowns. "Ask her."

Ashford turns to her, frowning. "What did I do wrong?"

"I hate having my hair pulled. It totally killed our scene."

"Why didn't you tell me that before we started?" he demands in frustration.

"You didn't ask."

I notice all of the trainers scribbling in their notebooks.

Once he is finished writing, Master Nosh looks up and tells Ashford, "Apologize to your submissive and ask if she would like to continue."

Ashford sighs, looking humiliated, but immediately complies. "I'm sorry I didn't ask before. Would you like to finish the scene?"

She nods. "Yes, Prince Ashford."

I smirk, amused by the title he's given himself.

Master Nosh calls out to the rest of us, "Proceed with your scenes."

I turn my attention back to my submissive, appreciating the importance of this practicum. Unwilling to cross her limits, I check in several times throughout our spanking session to make sure I'm not swatting her too aggressively.

Once her entire ass is a lovely light pink hue, I slip my hand between her legs and am gratified to find her pussy is wet.

I growl hungrily. "I'm going to lick my lollipop before I claim her."

"Please, Sir," she cries, moaning with pleasure as she

tilts her hips forward to give me greater access to her pussy.

I lean down to take a long lick, groaning when I taste her excitement. I then begin flicking her clit with my tongue and listen to her moan even louder. Losing myself in the pleasure of eating her pussy, I'm surprised by the sound of a man clearing his throat.

I look up and see the bald trainer standing beside me, motioning to his watch.

Wishing we had more time, I quickly stand up and unzip my pants. I hear her soft moan when I press my hard shaft against her wet opening.

"Lollipop, are you ready to be claimed?"

"Oh yes, Sir…" she says seductively, glancing back at me.

I thrust my cock into her and groan in pleasure when I feel her tight pussy conform to my shaft. Grasping her waist with both hands, I thrust into her and am rewarded by her loud cries of pleasure.

"Just how hard do you want it?" I ask, giving her a deep thrust.

"Really, *really* hard," she pants hungrily.

Granting my submissive's wish, I stroke her hard and deep, forcing her to take all of me. I glance at the mirrored wall beside us and watch as she takes each and every stroke.

Lollipop responds to my vigorous pounding by begging me for more. No longer aware of anyone else, I concentrate my attention on her, determined to indulge her carnal desire.

However, I want her to climax with me, so I suddenly stop. Leaning forward, I begin rubbing her clit while her pussy tightens around my shaft. Sensing when she's about to climax, I slap her ass soundly and command, "Come for me."

She nods, moaning when I start pumping her again…

When I find myself just on the brink of climax, I stop my thrusts again and groan as my cock releases inside her. When her own powerful climax takes over, the grateful sounds of her passionate cries fill the air.

I lean forward and turn her head to claim those pink lips while her inner muscles tremble in ecstasy.

I don't stop kissing her until they cease.

Lessons in Leadership

After the seven of us are dressed and the submissives have left the room, the instructors tell us to stand before the panel to receive our evaluations.

As I walk up to the table, Slater gives me a sideways glance and starts snickering under his breath.

I narrow my eyes, having no patience for his immaturity.

However, I notice the bearded trainer looking at me with amusement while he discreetly rubs his chin. I quickly glance at the mirrored wall.

To my mortification, I see that my face is smeared with bright pink lipstick, making me look like a horny teenage boy after a make-out session.

There's a reason I don't care for overdone makeup…

I quickly rub it off with the back of my hand and stand there, sighing inwardly.

Master Nosh, the Head Trainer, stands up to address us. "Before we begin the formal evaluation, let me introduce you to your panel of trainers." He points to the bald man standing beside him. "This is Vendari Steele." He then gestures to a distinguished gentleman with pale blue eyes sitting next to Steele. "And this is Maestro Leo."

The man nods to us.

Master Nosh introduces the trainer at the end who has the look and physique of a lumberjack and the beard to go with it. I detect reverence in his voice when he says, "This is Laird."

The redheaded man grins at us. "I'm looking forward to the next six weeks." Laird's friendly demeanor stands in stark contrast to the other trainers, who have countenances that are more serious and intimidating.

Master Nosh sits down and folds his arms, his gaze harsh as he continues to speak to us.

"We noticed something during the practicum that is quite concerning. Although the experienced submissives we partnered with you agreed to play out the scene as you directed, many of you overstepped your bounds tonight."

I swallow hard, wondering if I unknowingly made a mistake.

Master Nosh raises an eyebrow. "Many wannabe Doms assume that every scene ends with intercourse." He shakes his head. "That is a foolish assumption."

He addresses Ravenson first. "However, Mr. Ravenson, you did not have intercourse. Why is that?"

"I asked her what she wanted, and she made it clear she was only interested in being spanked."

Maestro Leo interjects, "You did exactly what was expected. Well done."

Vendari Steele then asks Ravenson, "How did it feel to scene with a submissive outside your preferred wheelhouse?"

Ravenson shifts uncomfortably before answering. "I'll admit, I'm not normally attracted to curvy women, but…I definitely enjoyed how her flesh rippled when I spanked her. It was erotic to watch."

Steele nods in agreement. "I have found that it is the chemistry between a Dominant and their submissive that yields the most pleasure—not the person's physical appearance."

"Point well taken," Ravenson concedes.

Master Nosh turns to Ashford next. "You failed to ask the questions needed which led to your submissive having to call out her safeword."

Ashford looks down at the floor, mumbling, "I'm well aware…"

Master Nosh demands sternly, "What have you learned, Mr. Ashford?"

He lets out a long sigh before answering. "I assumed that since it was a simple scene, it was pretty straightforward what I needed to do and forgot to ask about her limits. But, I thought all women like having their hair pulled."

The Head Trainer narrows his eyes. "Now you know of at least one who does not."

Standing beside Ashford, I can hear him grinding his teeth.

"Before the practicum, we gave you explicit instructions to apply what you learned," Laird reminds him, then adds with a wink, "Remember that next time."

Master Nosh turns to the man who took his submissive directly to the spanking bench and looks at him with displeasure. "Do you understand the seriousness of what you did wrong, Mr. Jones?"

The guy frowns. "I asked if she liked to be spanked and she said she did."

"What do you know about her other than that?" the Head Trainer demands.

He doesn't answer.

"Surely, you know something?" Maestro Leo barks.

Jones shakes his head, growling in anger. "She's not my type. I just wanted to get through the assignment."

"You just wanted to get through the assignment…" Maestro Leo repeats, glaring at the man. "Yet, you still had intercourse with her?"

Jones shrugs, mumbling, "Yeah…I figured that's the reward for doing the scene."

"The *reward* is the power exchange itself," Maestro Leo corrects him. "Intercourse is never a given. That is something to be negotiated prior to a scene."

Jones points his finger at me. "Why are you giving me a hard time when we all had to wait for *that* guy to finish fucking his submissive?"

All eyes turn to me.

"Mr. Davis, would you like to answer his question?" Vendari Steele asks.

I nod to the trainer before turning to answer Jones. "My submissive mentioned that she liked to be penetrated. When I asked her specifically if that's what she wanted, she confirmed it with me." I look at the four trainers, stating in my defense, "I had no idea we couldn't."

"No parameters were limiting your interaction," Master Nosh assures me. "The only limitations were the ones set by the submissives themselves."

Vendari Steele frowns, addressing the other students. "How many of you asked your submissive if they wanted to end the scene with intercourse?"

Shockingly, not one raises their hand, not even Miss Reid, who'd leaned against the spanking bench and ordered her male submissive to fuck her.

"Our experienced submissives understood the lesson we were teaching tonight and were well aware that many of you would fail to ask them," Master Nosh informs us. "You can rest assured that if they had been unwilling, they would have called their safeword before penetration."

But, before any of us can relax, Master Nosh warns us in a grave tone, "Moving forward, do *not* count on safewords as your failsafe. There is no excuse as a Dominant for a lack of communication between you and your sub. Have I made myself clear?"

"Yes," we answer in unison.

Maestro Leo explains, "The submissives you will work with during this course have extensive training and deserve nothing but your utmost respect. We purposely chose partners tonight that would challenge the preconceived preferences you listed in your application. One of the main objectives of tonight's practicum was to open your eyes to opportunities you may have been blind to before."

I appreciate his point. I certainly wouldn't have given

lollipop a second glance if I were at a BDSM club because of her flamboyant makeup. And, yet, we had an exceedingly enjoyable scene together.

The Head Trainer turns back to me and continues his evaluation. "Mr. Davis, you were thorough in your questions before the scene, but you also listened to your submissive's wishes and, because of that, you were able to enhance her experience tonight."

"However," Maestro Leo says, raising a finger, "I noticed that you were overly cautious while spanking her."

"She'd mentioned that she had a low tolerance for pain," I explain.

"I understand. However, you checked in far too often during your scene even though she repeatedly indicated that she was enjoying the level of impact. At what point do you trust her?"

"I didn't want to make a mistake," I answer defensively.

"This isn't a paper exam to be filled out. You must trust your submissive as well as your instincts," he remarks.

I nod, accepting his criticism, and realize Marquis Gray shared the same advice earlier this night.

Trust your instincts…

After the evaluations are over, the trainers instruct us to go to the commons area and enjoy a quick bite while we wait for our second practicum of the evening.

The seven of us enter the area in silence, still digesting the feedback we've received. Not interested in food, I sit down at a round table while the rest fill up small plates with savory appetizers.

Miss Reid is the first to walk over to my table and join me. "Not hungry?" she asks as she picks up a small sandwich from her plate.

"Too hyped to eat," I admit.

She nods as she chews and waits until she swallows to hold out her hand to me. "I'm Kat, by the way."

"Thane," I answer, shaking her hand firmly.

She looks at her sandwich, shaking her head. "I wonder what the trainers have planned for us next."

"No idea," I chuckle.

Ravenson and the loner, Ashford, come over to join us.

"What are you two talking about?" Ravenson asks, taking a seat beside me.

"We were wondering what the trainers have up their sleeves for this next practicum," Kat tells him.

Ravenson snorts. "I consider myself fortunate to have gotten out of that first one unscathed."

Kat eyes both of us. "Yeah, the two of you sailed through it with flying colors. But, just so you know, it didn't go unnoticed…" She nods at the other side of the commons.

I glance over to see the other three huddled together and catch Slater, i.e. Surfer Boy, glaring at me.

Jones slaps him on the shoulder to get his attention and Slater immediately looks away.

I can tell that Jones is still upset about being called out by the trainers. Although I can't hear what he's saying, the man is very animated when he talks, and he keeps pounding his fist into his hand.

"I don't think that guy is going to last long," Miss Reid murmurs darkly.

Ravenson looks over at Jones and frowns. "I bet the trainers are watching him closely."

I nod in agreement.

Kat holds out her hand to Ravenson. "So, I'm Kat."

He replies with a courteous smile, "I'm Samuel."

"Can I call you Sam?"

He furrows his brow. "Certainly not!"

"That's the reason I asked," she laughs, turning to Ashford. "And, you?"

He looks up from his plate of food. "Huh?"

"What's your first name?"

"Ashford."

She snickers. "So, you're telling me your parents named you Ashford Ashford, did they?"

"No," he mutters, pushing his glasses back up before diving back into his food.

I appreciate Kat's wit and chill manner. It helps to pass the time while we all wait for our next challenge.

When I glance over at Jones again, I'm relieved to see he's calmed down some.

Surfer Boy suddenly looks up and smiles at me.

It's the kind of smile that lets me know he's up to no good.

Master Nosh walks into the commons while the others are still eating. I immediately stand up, assuming he's come to direct us to the second practicum. However, he walks past me as he heads over to the group of three on the opposite side of the commons.

"Come to my office, Mr. Jones." The tone in the Head Trainer's voice leaves no room for dissent, and the man follows him out of the commons in silence.

"What do you think's happening?" Kat whispers after the two leave.

"I'm certain we already know," I answer somberly.

Being accepted into the Dominant Training program gave us all a sense of privilege, but tonight is proof that we are very much expendable.

Twenty minutes later, Master Nosh arrives without Jones and escorts us to the auditorium. No one says a word as we walk down the hallway.

It is sobering to know we can be cut from the program at any moment, but I can see the genius behind it, too. When you know this opportunity is something you can lose, you will work that much harder for it.

As we enter the auditorium, I'm surprised to find it's circular, with a small stage in the center and rows of seats all around it. The other instructors are already seated and waiting for us.

Master Nosh leads us down to the center stage and gestures for us to take a seat in the front row.

Before he joins the other trainers, he stands before

us and says, "I'm sure you have noticed you have one less classmate in your ranks. It is important that you understand why."

The entire auditorium becomes eerily silent.

"Mr. Jones was under the false impression that his needs were more important than his submissive's. It became evident to all of us during the first practicum. Upon further discussion with the man, I've concluded that not only is he a poor fit for the Training Center, but that he is also not ready to become a Dominant."

I hear a sharp intake of breath from several of my classmates.

"The role of a Dominant is a challenging one," Master Nosh warns us. "It is not about using submissives for your pleasure with no regard to their wellbeing. That is an immature and dangerous misconception."

He folds his arms. "Being a Dominant requires respect. You must respect a submissive's free will and their right to say no. Even in a Master/slave dynamic, where the submissive has agreed to be used as a vessel of pleasure in whatever way their Master sees fit, the slave must agree to that role and can revoke it at any time."

Master Nosh looks at each of us somberly. "Failure to understand and embrace that fact makes a person unfit to be a Dominant. If you have an issue with that fundamental truth, we ask that you leave now. As with the last two who were dismissed, your money will be fully refunded."

No one makes a move.

"Understand that by remaining here, you are committing to respect every submissive you come in contact with. Even if they fail to respect you."

"Wait! There's no way I am going to sit back and take their disrespect," Lofton objects.

"We are not asking you to, Mr. Lofton. However, you cannot gain respect by being disrespectful in return."

Addressing all of us, Master Nosh explains, "The best way to handle disrespect from a submissive you are unfamiliar with is to keep calm and remain civil while you remove yourself from their presence."

Master Nosh furrows his brow. "If you cannot do that simple task, you have no business being here."

The Head Trainer's next words resonate in my soul. "As a Dominant, you have *chosen* to take on the role of a leader. Therefore, it is your duty to act as one."

I am struck once more by the profound lessons being taught here tonight. I naturally assumed the trainers would ease us into the course on the first day.

Instead, they seem determined to challenge us at every turn.

Electrify Me

Laird stands up and starts clapping his hands. "Congratulations students, you have made it to your second practicum of the evening. We're excited for you because, for the next six weeks, you will have the unprecedented opportunity to learn from the renowned dominants who specialize in specific tools and techniques."

While he speaks, several staff members appear on stage, carrying a long table. They are followed by a line of submissives who lay out six boxes in a row.

I watch in stunned silence as three bondage tables are lowered from the ceiling above. The execution of this scene change feels like a high-end theater production rather than a BDSM class.

Laird walks up the stairs of the stage and heads to the long table. "Tonight, you will learn the secrets of the violet wand." He smirks when he adds, "Which is not to be confused with a 'violent' wand."

I chuckle, along with several of my classmates.

Laird gestures to the right as he makes his introduction, "Viscount Killian will be instructing you on its use. Our distinguished guest has over twenty years of experience with the violet wand and has traveled the world to demonstrate his skill with the instrument at the request of Dominants and submissives alike."

A man dressed all in black walks onto the stairs. He is toting a black case.

Laird holds out his hand to the Viscount, who shakes it firmly.

"We are honored you have come to share your knowledge with us tonight, sir."

Once Laird leaves the stage, the Viscount sets his case on the table and turns to address our class.

"After tonight, you will understand why this is my favorite stimulation tool."

Opening his case, Viscount Killian takes out a wand with a glass attachment and inserts the plug into an outlet on the floor. The lights in the auditorium suddenly darken as he holds up the wand as if it were a torch.

The moment he turns it on, the air buzzes with a pleasant humming sound while the glass attachment lights up with a purple electrical current.

I smile in appreciation. I've seen the tool used before at the BDSM clubs I frequent, but I have yet to use the tool myself.

"The violet wand is basically a modified Tesla coil," he informs us. "The electrodes are generally made of clear tempered glass with a noble gas inside, typically argon.

"The high voltage current causes the plasma inside to

become excited and emit the glowing purple color." He strokes the length of the glass with his finger, and it crackles with electricity. "When the electrode gets near the skin or any conductive surface, tiny bolts of static electricity jump between the two and creates a sensation that can be as light as a tickle or as sharp as the blade of a knife being dragged across your skin."

He runs the wand down his arm. "If the electrode is touching the surface of the skin, it will have a minimal effect. But…" He starts to pull the instrument away from his skin and smiles. "…as you move it farther away, the intensity of the spark will increase."

Pointing to the glass electrode attached to the wand, he explains, "This mushroom-shaped electrode is wider, so it spreads the shock across a larger area and stings less."

The Viscount turns off the wand and sets it down. Then he pulls out a new glass attachment from his case. Rather than the shape of a mushroom, this one has a pointed end. "This electrode concentrates the shock to make it feel even more intense."

Putting it back in the case, he picks up one in the shape of a comb and says with a mischievous grin, "This electrode is particularly fun because it spreads the electricity across each of the teeth, hitting multiple points all at once."

Viscount Killian carefully sets it back into his case and pulls out a small, multi-tailed whip. "This is an electro whip attachment. It's made of highly conductive silicone. When you use it to flog your partner, it will produce an electric shock that is quite stimulating!"

He sets the whip attachment down and picks up a cord with a flat metal plate.

"But this…" he says with reverence. "…this is my favorite attachment. I know it looks unimpressive compared to the flogger, but this baby will transform you into a living electrode."

He holds up the connection end. "First, you attach the body contact cable to the wand while it's turned off. Then you place this metal piece against your skin. You can slip it either inside a bra or a waistband, like so…"

He lifts up his shirt and slips the flat metal piece between the waistband of his pants and his skin. Then Viscount Killian turns the wand back on…

Nothing seems to be happening, although I can hear a faint humming sound.

He grins in excitement. "Now, whenever you touch your partner, they will receive an electric shock. Just imagine the erotic things you can make your submissive feel when you explore their body with your electrified touch. You can tease and please them by varying the distance of your fingers from their skin, thereby creating different levels of intensity for them to enjoy. And, if you use the violet wand on sensitive areas like the neck, inner thighs, or behind the knees…"

He chuckles wickedly. "You can create an *intensely* pleasurable sensation."

Raising his eyebrows suggestively, he tells us, "I recommend teasing your partner's nipples by hovering your fingers directly over their breasts. However, you are not only limited to touch, my friends. You can also give them mind-blowing oral sex!"

The Viscount laughs gleefully. "They'll never forget how you made them come with your electric tongue."

Several of my classmates join in his laughter.

Grinning, he tells us, "Even kisses become more intense when sparks and ticklish sensations flow between your lips and theirs."

I shift in my seat, finding the idea arousing.

"Of course," he states in a somber tone, "it is important to keep in mind that this entertaining tool is still an electrical unit. Although it uses minuscule amperage, you should *never* use it on anyone who has a pacemaker or an erratic heartbeat."

He turns off the humming wand and sets it down, then quickly rattles off a number of other warnings, as well as several mistakes that are important to avoid.

"Listen very carefully, because I say this from personal experience. *Always* turn off the violet wand whenever you are switching attachments. If you forget, you might find yourself screaming like a little girl."

He glances at Kat. "I mean no offense, Miss Reid."

Kat smiles back at him. "None taken."

He grins proudly when he addresses the group, "I have brought each of you a violet wand set. I want you to practice using them on each other."

"Each other?" Lofton complains. "Can't we practice with a sub?"

Viscount Killian declares firmly, "Absolutely not! The only way for you to learn how to properly use this tool is to experiment on yourselves."

We all stand up, and I wait behind Reid while the others walk to the stage to claim one of the boxes. She turns around and asks me, "Want to be my partner?"

"Certainly."

As we head to the table, Slater intercepts her and opens his shirt wide. "Hey, you want to practice on this manly chest?"

"Nope, I already have a partner."

He frowns. "Who?"

Reid nods to me and continues toward the table to get her box.

Slater gives me a deadly look. "Dick."

I snort in amusement as I walk past him to grab the last remaining box. Opening the lid, I count five different glass attachments in addition to the violet wand itself.

"Come over here," Reid calls out to me, having already claimed one of the bondage tables.

"Lucky prick," Ravenson jokes, glancing in Kat's direction. "You get to work with her, while I have to partner with Ashford Ashford."

I chuckle, finding it humorous that Kat's nickname for the guy has already stuck. Heading over to her, I nearly drop my box of glass instruments when Slater slams into me.

"Watch where you're going, man!" he yells. "You almost made me drop my box."

"Watch yourself…" I growl in irritation.

"You'll need to be more careful with that," Viscount Killian cautions me from across the stage.

I look up to find all the trainers staring at me. I'm certain they didn't see what just happened.

I glance at Slater. He has his back to the trainers, and he is jeering at me.

Rolling my eyes, I walk to the table, gripping my box tightly with both hands.

Kat has already taken out her wand and attached the mushroom-shaped electrode. Plugging it in, she raises an eyebrow. "Are you ready for me to electrify you, Mr. Davis?"

"Why not?" I'm curious about how it will feel and set my box down. Taking off my jacket and tie first, I quickly unbutton my dress shirt and lay all three in a neat pile.

Standing before her bare-chested, I hold out my arms and ask, "Where would you like to start, Miss Reid?"

She says with an impish smile, "We'll start with those muscular arms, and then I'll work my way down to those sensitive areas the Viscount told us about."

Kat and I spend the next few hours exploring the different sensations and levels of intensity we can create using the multiple electrodes. I feel like I'm back in college and working in a science lab as we test the limits of the wand and our own pain preferences under Viscount Killian's watchful eye.

By the time the two of us are done, both Kat and I have stripped down to our underwear, wanting to explore each other's bodies with the violet wand. All, except for our lips.

"Are you curious about the electrified kiss?" she asks me.

"I am," I admit without hesitation.

"Me, too!"

I open my box and insert the attachment into the

wand, slipping the metal plate into the waistband of my boxers. Switching it on, I turn to face her.

"Ready?"

"Give it to me, Mr. Davis."

It feels odd to kiss a fellow Dominant, but my curiosity drives me on. Leaning forward, I move in for the kiss and feel an interesting electrical shock when our lips meet.

Kat's eyes widen, letting me know she feels it, too. I give her an even deeper kiss and don't pull away until my lips start to tingle. I now have a much clearer idea of what going down on a woman might feel like, and I look forward to trying it out with a sub.

After turning off the device, Viscount Killian walks up and slaps both of us on the backs. "Fun, isn't it?"

Kat nods. "I completely understand why this is your favorite tool."

I carefully place the wand back in the box, telling him, "Thank you for letting us experiment with your wands."

He laughs. "They're yours to keep. You'll need to bring it with you tomorrow for your first practicum."

I shake his hand, moved by his generosity. "Thank you."

"Use it in good health, Mr. Davis," he chuckles. "And, if you ever have questions, don't hesitate to call and ask."

He turns to the other students. "That goes for all of you."

I don't arrive back at my apartment until almost two in the morning. Even though I need to get up by five o'clock to get ready for work, I find I'm way too wired to fall asleep.

I know the six weeks ahead are going to be hell to survive. Still, I can't wait for the next class.

Friends

Anton Durov surprises me with a call at work the next day. "*Moy droog,* what do you say to dropping everything to spend the day with me?"

I chuckle. "Much as I want to, I can't take off to Russia."

"You always give me the same excuse when I ask you. Work, work, work."

"What can I say? It's my reality."

"What about flying out this weekend, then?"

"Sorry, I just started the Dominant Training course. I literally have no time right now."

"Tell me more about this Dominant Training class," he says with interest.

I tell him excitedly, "It's more than I hoped it would be, Durov." Glancing at my watch again, I sigh. "But I have to go. I'll call you tonight and give you all the details."

"Fine," he chuckles. "We'll talk later."

I go back to work, losing myself in my current assignment, which is why I nearly jump out of my skin when I hear Durov's voice behind me a few minutes later.

"Are you ready to talk now, *moy droog?*"

Spinning around in my chair, I'm stunned to see the burly Russian standing in my tiny cubicle.

He grins. "Is that a no, then, comrade?"

I shoot out of my chair and clasp his shoulder, thrilled to see him. "I can't believe you're here!"

He smirks. "Live and in the flesh."

I shake my head in disbelief. "What are you doing in the US?"

Durov gives me a troubled look and shakes his head.

He is like a brother to me. Sensing something's wrong, I drop everything and ask my boss for time off.

Minutes later, I return from his office and grab my jacket. "I'm free for the rest of the day. Where to?"

He grins. "The beach, *moy droog.*"

Durov insists I ride with him. I notice he has an entourage of men for protection going everywhere with us. When I ask him what's wrong, he ignores the question and asks, "When was the last time you've been to the beach, comrade?"

I laughingly admit, "It's been a while."

"You realize without me in your life, you have none."

I smirk. "Normally, I would agree, but not after starting this course."

Durov drives us to the beach house he keeps here in the States and, over vodka, gives me a summary of his troubles back in Russia, but then quickly changes the subject. "Tell me more about this class you're taking."

Standing at the kitchen counter, I give Durov a complete rundown, beginning with my first run-in with Surfer Boy in the parking lot.

"The boy sounds annoying. Do you need me to take him out?"

"No need," I laugh. "I think I can handle the jerk."

After telling him about the spanking practicum, I attempt to lighten his mood by making a joke. "You know, it's surprising that a simple spanking scene could have so many impactful lessons."

Durov breaks out in a smile as he pours us another round. "I see what you did there, *moy droog*. Impactful lessons, indeed…"

I shake my head and grin when I tell him, "These trainers don't let anything slide. I mean, we lost two students before the first night even ended."

"I respect the trainers' ruthlessness," Durov states with a smirk.

Still riding on the emotional high of the whole experience, I tell him, "They don't let up, not for one second. If last night was any indication, this course is everything I was hoping for—and more."

"I'm glad to hear it, comrade. Truly."

Thinking he might enjoy the violet wand, I ask, "Have you ever used a violet wand before?"

"*Nyet,* but I have used cattle prods."

I burst out laughing. "Of course you have, you fucking sadist."

Durov grins. "Tell me more about this electric wand, *moy droog.*"

Knowing that he's genuinely interested, I go on to tell him about my experience testing out the instrument, including my electrified kiss with Kat.

He raises an eyebrow. "What was that like?"

"Like nothing I've ever experienced before. It was crazy to literally feel a bolt of electricity when I kissed her on the lips."

He smirks. "Was it just the wand, *moy droog?*"

I roll my eyes, knowing what he is implying. "Reid and I were simply curious. Nothing more to it, I assure you." Quickly changing the subject, I ask, "Do you realize that by the time I am done with the course, I will know more and have experienced more than most Doms do in a lifetime?"

He nods, grinning at me. "I knew the Training Center would suit you."

Not wanting him to miss out, I offer, "Would you like me to talk to them about letting you join a future session?"

"*Nyet.* I prefer to stick with my cat o' nines, but I'm glad you are enjoying yourself."

We spend the entire day relaxing on the beach. After everything Durov has gone through back in Russia, it's obvious that being next to the ocean has a healing effect on his soul.

Later, when it's nearly time for me to leave for class, I regretfully tell him I need to go.

"Can't you skip one night, *moy droog?*"

I shake my head. "I can't. Every class covers something new. But why don't you come with me tonight?" I suggest. "They always have activities going on there."

Durov agrees to check out the place. He drops me off at work and has his men follow my car to the Training Center while he rides with me.

While I'm on the road, my phone starts to ring. I glance down to see it's my old college roommate, Brad Anderson. Not wanting to be distracted while I'm driving, I wait until I reach the parking lot to flip my phone open and call him back.

"Things are a bit crazy for me right now," I tell him, motioning to Durov that I'll be a minute and he should go on.

"I'm sorry to hear that buddy," Anderson says, sounding concerned.

I laugh. "Actually, things are going well. I just don't have a minute to myself."

"Why's that?"

"I finally bit the bullet and started the Dominant Training course."

"About time! So, I take it you're enjoying yourself?"

"The course is even better than I expected."

"That's really saying something. I know how you are…"

"What are you implying?" I tease him.

Anderson chuckles. "Just that you're a man with exceedingly high expectations."

"I'm happy to report that the trainers have not only met those expectations but surpassed them." I glance down at my watch. "Unfortunately, I've got to head into class right now. Was there something you wanted?"

"There is, actually. Morning Wood Ranch caught the attention of a major grocery distributor in California, and my pop wants me to fly out to meet with them. I know it's awfully late notice, but I was wondering if I could stay with you."

"My place isn't much, but you're certainly welcome to stay here."

"Thanks, and I'll make you a deal," Anderson tells me. "I'll do all the cooking while I'm there."

"No need," I assure him. "I'm happy to have you."

"I insist, buddy. Do you have any idea how much a hotel costs for a week's stay in LA? It's like a freaking house payment. I just can't see throwing that kind of money away."

"It is ridiculous," I agree, laughing. "You know, I'm glad you're coming. Between work and this course, I'm hardly home these days. At least now, someone will be using the apartment."

"Just one more thing before I let you go."

I glance at my watch again and see I only have ten minutes before class starts. Getting out of the car, I pull out my tool bag from the back seat to join Durov at the entrance of the building.

"What is it, Anderson?"

"I'll be flying in on Sunday. Is that going to be a problem?"

I smile. "You're actually in luck. Sunday is the only day I have off, so I can pick you up at the airport and save you the cab fare."

"No need to go to any trouble. Letting me stay at your apartment is more than enough."

"I already have it all planned out," I tell him. "Bring your swim trunks. We'll be heading to the beach straight from the airport."

"Well, hot dang! Now, that's an offer I can't refuse. See you soon."

I hang up and walk up to the reception desk to introduce Durov.

Miss Dunningham smiles. "Oh, I remember Rytsar Durov, Mr. Davis."

S She turns to him. "It's a pleasure to see you again. Are you here for the demonstrations? If so, I can get you a pamphlet highlighting tonight's performances as well as your visitor pass."

Durov smiles charmingly. "Visitor pass—yes. But no need for a pamphlet."

She blushes, signing him in and handing him the pass. "Enjoy!" When he takes the pass and winks at her, her blush grows even deeper.

I slap Durov on the shoulder. "I've seriously got to go. Want to meet in the parking lot after my class is over?"

He grins. "No need, *moy droog*. I don't plan to stay long."

I get the sense that spending the day on the beach was just what the Russian needed. Heck, if I'm being honest. I needed it, too.

Chastity

After getting off the elevator, I rush down the hallway and make it to class just as the bell rings. All eyes turn to me as I sit down—including our instructor's.

"Alana, I apologize for being late. A good friend called and needed a favor."

She nods, stating, "Friends and family are important."

Turning to the class, Alana takes the opportunity to speak on the subject. "As a Dominant, it is easy to become overly self-reliant. Be cautious about that. It's important to create a circle of people you can trust and rely on."

She smiles when she adds, "Take it from me, it will serve you well in countless ways in the years to come."

I'm grateful to Alana for being understanding. The last thing I want is to disrespect her or her time.

Ready to get to work, I pull out my notebook. As Alana launches into the lesson, I begin taking notes, but even as I start writing down the importance of providing aftercare for a submissive, my mind drifts back to Anderson. The guy's timing couldn't be worse for a visit, but I seriously can't wait to see him.

By the end of class, I am itching to begin the first practicum.

Alana informs us, "Now that you've had a chance to practice on yourselves, we want you to have an opportunity to use the violet wand in a scene. Naturally, we also expect you to apply what you learned about aftercare."

As I'm walking down the hallway toward the next practicum, Surfer Boy slides up beside me and mutters under his breath, "I see how it is…"

"What?" I snarl, walking faster.

"You've got her eating out of your hand. Is it possible you're shagging our good professor outside of class?"

Offended that he would slander Alana's good name, I take a sudden, spontaneous swing at him.

Slater dodges my punch but smirks as he raises his hands in surrender and backs away. In a low voice only I can hear, he taunts, "Methinks the lady doth protest too much…"

"Mr. Davis!"

I look down the hallway to see Master Nosh staring hard at me.

This is the second time Slater has made me look like the aggressor. I keep quiet because I know anything I say in my own defense will only make things worse.

I have no idea why Slater is pushing my buttons, but the guy is a fool if he thinks I'm going to do anything to jeopardize this opportunity. I smile to myself because Surfer Boy has no idea who he's dealing with. I've survived my monstrous mother, so this…well, this is just a walk in the park for me.

I walk up to Master Nosh and assure him that it will not happen again.

"No, it will not," the Head Trainer agrees harshly. "We have no tolerance for violent behavior at this school."

I'm grateful for my ability to compartmentalize problems. Rather than stew over Slater's latest stunt, I focus all my energy on the task at hand—which happens to be a pleasurable one.

This practicum is being held in a larger room than the one from last night. I notice six tantra chairs spaced far apart as I walk in. The other trainers are sitting at a table in the center of the room.

Walking over to the table, Master Nosh sits down and reminds us, "Tonight, we will observe how you utilize what you've learned about the violet wand. As you can see, we have spaced the tantra chairs out to prevent unintentional arcs from your instruments during the scenes."

I chuckle to myself, thinking how funny it would be if we accidentally shocked each other while wielding our violet wands for the first time with a sub. Damn, that would be fucking hilarious!

Maestro Leo tells the class, "Once again, you will be scening with a submissive who has been specifically chosen for you based on the application you filled out."

Laird assigns us each a tantra chair and tells us to set

up our wands and prepare ourselves while we wait for our submissives to arrive. I'm curious to see who they have chosen for me this time.

I take off my jacket and shirt, then remove my belt with its metal clasp to prevent any unwanted shocks. I set out the wand with the mushroom-shaped attachment to start my scene.

That done, I stand with my arms behind my back as I wait for the submissives to enter the room. When they finally arrive, they immediately bow before the panel of trainers and wait for their command.

I noticed that this time, all of the submissives are women.

"Join your partner for the evening," Master Nosh orders.

I watch as a young woman with an innocent face and a head full of honey-colored curls walks up to me wearing a sweet smile.

The trainers did right by me.

When asked what type of partner I'm attracted to, I'd written, "The girl next door." The submissive approaching me tonight is the very personification of that wish.

She lowers her eyes respectfully before bowing at my feet. "How may I serve you tonight?" she asks in a pleasant tone.

I place my hand on her head, formally accepting her submission for the evening. "Stand and look at me."

She moves gracefully as she stands up. I suck in my breath when I gaze into her blue eyes. William Shakespeare said that the eyes were the windows to the soul, and what I see before me is a pure soul.

"Is there a name you would like me to call you by for tonight's scene?"

"Chastity."

I smile. "Does that define your spirit or your intentions?"

Her cheeks blush a pretty pink. "Both."

I cock my head. "How so?"

"I approach every experience with an open mind. However, I am waiting until I'm collared before I give my maidenhood to another."

"You are still a virgin?" I ask, wanting to be clear.

She stares at my bare chest when she answers. "I am."

Understanding her boundary, I follow up with another question. "Does the same rule apply to your ass?"

"It does," she answers.

"And your throat?"

She nods and looks at me apprehensively. "Is that a problem?"

"No, I find it intriguing," I assure her. Now that I know there will be no penetration, I make a mental adjustment to the scene I will be playing out. "How long have you been a submissive?"

"Three years."

Glancing at the wand sitting on the small table, I ask her, "Have you scened with a violet wand before?"

She shakes her head with a smile. "I have not."

"So, you are a virgin in that sense, too?"

Her eyes sparkle. "Yes."

I raise an eyebrow. "Then I look forward to deflowering you tonight in that area only."

Now that the parameters have been set, I am ready to begin. "Tonight, you will address me as Sir."

"It will be my pleasure, Sir."

"Strip for me, chastity, including all of your jewelry."

I watch with satisfaction as chastity slowly unveils her body before me. I find it charming that her nipples are as pink as her lips.

"Turn for me," I command, staring at her pussy.

Chastity slowly turns, showing off her firm ass.

"You are lovely," I tell her in a low voice as I reach out to caress her soft skin.

"Thank you, Sir."

There is something alluring about the fact that I cannot claim her. Rather than finding it frustrating, I am turned on by the prospect. I want to protect her innocence even while I introduce her to the erotic stimulation of the violet wand.

I order her to lie down on the tantra chair with her legs spread.

She does so and looks up at me expectantly.

Out of the corner of my eye, I notice one of the trainers standing nearby silently observing us. Not wanting his presence to affect our scene, I keep my attention solely on her.

"First, we will start with a light tickle, and I'll increase the intensity from there. If at any time it becomes too much, I want you to call out your safeword. 'Yellow' if you want me to continue at a lower setting or 'red' if you want me to stop."

After the trainers' last evaluation, I've decided against constantly checking in. After all, I don't wish to distract my submissive from enjoying our scene together. Instead, I've given her the power to direct me if she becomes uncomfortable at any point.

Naturally, I still plan to watch for any signs that might indicate distress. However, since we're new to each other, doing it this way eliminates any temptation I might have to constantly second guess myself.

I pick up the violet wand and turn it on its lowest setting. It starts to glow with its purple light while it hums softly.

Chastity's eyes widen in fear and excitement as I place the glass electrode on her stomach and lightly trace it over her skin. "Do you like that?"

I watch in satisfaction when she smiles, exclaiming, "I do! I never thought electricity could tickle."

I make several passes over her body, enjoying the sound of her delighted giggles. Then I turn up the power and ask, "Are you ready?"

"Absolutely," she answers confidently.

After several more passes, I quickly realize that the mushroom-shaped electrode is not enough stimulation for her, even when I set it at its highest setting. Trading out the electrode, I move on to the comb with its multiple points of contact.

Chastity responds well to it and begs me to keep turning up the power. I trail the points of the comb slowly up her inner thigh and watch her body tremble as I get ever closer to her virginal pussy. When I feel I've teased her enough, I decide to change things up.

"Do you enjoy floggers?"

Her eyes light up. "Yes!"

I hold out the whip attachment to show her. "Although it's small and I'm not an expert with the flogger, this little device can deliver a fun bite."

"I'm all in," she replies.

I enjoy her adventurous spirit. Turning off the wand, I replace the attachment and flick it back on. I start by dragging the multi-tailed instrument over her bare skin and watch the goosebumps start to rise as she responds to the electricity.

"I see you enjoy it," I murmur huskily.

"It feels amazing, Sir."

"Do you want me to turn up the power?"

"If it pleases you," she answers enthusiastically.

I turn it up, grazing her skin lightly to test her response to the amperage before commanding, "Turn around and lie against the high end of the chair. I want full access to your back and ass."

She readily complies.

I straddle the chair, positioning myself behind her, and begin lightly swinging the whip against her back. I listen to her excited gasps of pleasure. "Do you want me to turn it higher?"

"Oh, yes, Sir…" she moans.

Cranking it higher until the wand is really humming, I lace her back with the flogger. But she doesn't really start screaming in pleasure until I concentrate my attention on her firm little ass.

When I see her pussy dripping with excitement, I know that electricity is her kink. Needing to taste her, I give her one last spirited stroke with the flogger before turning off the wand.

Her whole body is trembling when I lean down to tell her, "I'm going to electrify my mouth and make you come."

"Oh, my God…" she whimpers excitedly.

I help her change positions so her back is lying against the top curve of the tantra chair and she is in a lovely arched pose with her legs spread wide open.

Switching out the flogger for the body conductor attachment, I slip the metal plate into my waistband and tell her, "This will be a first for both of us as I have never done this before."

"It's so hot knowing we are sharing this first together," she purrs.

Turning on the wand, I sit on the chair with my face in line with her wet pussy. Leaning forward, I take my first lick. We groan in unison, both of us responding to the tingling sensation caused by the current passing between my tongue and her virginal pussy.

Her tangy-sweet taste turns me on, and I growl with desire, "Don't hold back, chastity. I want to feel you orgasm against my tongue."

"Yes, Sir," she cries with excitement.

I lavish my attention on her pussy, flicking her clit with my electrified tongue. The jolt of electricity adds to the experience, and I lose myself in her pleasure. I don't let up until I feel her thighs quivering, announcing her climax. Laying my tongue flat against her pussy, I groan, feeling the tingling sensation of the electrical current as her inner muscles twitch.

"Oh, my God. Oh. My. *God!*" she screams, clutching my head as she comes.

I finally pull away, the electricity between us becoming too intense, and find her staring at me with luminous eyes. "That was magnificent…"

"It was," I agree, turning off the wand. I place it and the conductor on the floor before pulling her to me so I can ravage her mouth.

I hold her close afterward, murmuring words of praise as she comes down from the intense high of our encounter.

The truth is that I am flying on a high of my own in response to her enjoyment. Being able to give this virginal woman such profound satisfaction is deeply empowering.

There is nothing else like it!

I tenderly nibble her neck, saying with amusement, "It appears, dear chastity, that electricity turns you on."

Later that night, as I lie in bed with my eyes closed, I can't stop thinking about the encounter. Not just about the scene itself—but what happened afterward.

In my mind, I replay what each trainer said during my evaluation. All four trainers praised my choices throughout the scene with chastity, as well as my care afterward. I feel both humbled and inspired by their assessment.

Everything came naturally to me tonight. It left like breathing—as if this was what I was always meant to do.

But it wasn't until Maestro Leo's revelation after

class that I fully understood the trust they had placed in me.

As I was heading to my old beater car, the trainer hurried to catch up to me. "Mr. Davis, I want you to know that we had complete confidence in you."

"I appreciate that, Maestro Leo."

He looks at me thoughtfully. "There is something I didn't tell you, Mr. Davis."

My heart starts to race, certain the ax is about to fall.

"The young woman you scened with tonight…"

"Yes."

"She is Headmaster Kennedy's daughter."

"The headmaster of the entire Training Center?"

He nods.

I stare at him, dumbstruck, and watch him walk back into the school.

Holy hell, I didn't see that coming…

Perspective

I'm not prepared when I get a call from Master Nosh later in the week. "Mr. Davis, can you come in a half-hour earlier tonight? I need to speak to you privately."

"Of course."

After I hang up, I find myself struggling to concentrate at work. I keep wondering if it's about the latest incident with Surfer Boy. The evening before, he'd cornered me in the bathroom…

"Tell me, Davis. On a scale from one to ten, how would you rate our instructor as a fuck?"

"Get away from me, asshole," I'd growled. "I want nothing to do with you."

"Of course you don't. I'm the only one who's figured out what's really going on. Not only are you fucking our instructor, but you must give one hell of a blow job.

How else can you explain the way the trainers fawn all over you?"

Slater went to unbutton his pants. "Maybe if you suck *my* dick, I won't give a fuck, either."

Rather than give him the satisfaction of a reaction, I clamped my fists tight to stop myself from decking him in the jaw. Preserving my composure, I rushed out of the bathroom and almost hit one of the trainers with the damn door.

"Where's the fire?" Laird laughed good-naturedly.

I forced a smile. "Sorry, I didn't mean to almost take you out—"

Slater shoved the door open violently in pursuit of me. But, as soon as he saw Laird, he stopped short. Surfer Boy's demeanor completely changed in that moment, and he swiped his hair back, looking as if he'd been traumatized.

Without saying a word, he glanced briefly at the trainer and then started down the hallway with his hands in his pockets and his head lowered.

Laird watched him walk away, saying nothing, then headed in the opposite direction.

I didn't think any more of the incident—until now. What if Laird reported the incident to Master Nosh, which is the reason for this sudden meeting?

Needing to stay an hour longer to finish up at work, I'm forced to skip dinner and grab an apple on the way so I can make it to Nosh's meeting on time.

Rachael Dunningham looks up and smiles when she sees me. "Master Nosh is waiting for you in his office, Mr. Davis."

I nod to her, appreciating her pleasant demeanor since I am feeling far from confident as I make my way to the elevator. My stomach churning with uneasiness, I take a deep breath before lightly rapping on his office door.

"Come in, Mr. Davis," Master Nosh states, his tone dire.

I open the door to find him sitting behind a rustic pine desk. The office is minimally decorated, the focal point being a majestic portrait of a Native American with a single feather in his hair.

Master Nosh notices me staring at it and asks, "Do you know who he is?"

I shake my head, unfamiliar with Cheyenne history.

He stares at the portrait thoughtfully. "He was known as Little Wolf."

I carefully study the painting. The look of masculine confidence on the man's face strikes a chord in me. It almost feels as if he is a presence in this room.

"Little Wolf was a great leader of my people, and he is someone I continue to learn from."

I make a mental note to look into Little Wolf because of Master Nosh's open esteem of the man.

"Sit," the Head Trainer orders, gesturing to a chair beside the desk.

I sit down in the large chair, expecting him to ask about my run-ins with Slater.

Instead, Master Nosh surprises me. "I know Maestro Leo spoke to you about the Headmaster's daughter."

"He did," I reply, still reeling from that revelation.

"You need to know that as a student of the program, you represent the Training Center. Therefore, as one of our students, you are not allowed to fraternize with *any* of the submissives you partner with during your training, including the Headmaster's daughter," he informs me. "Not here at the Center, nor outside these walls."

I stare at him in surprise. "Why?"

"Anything less than your full commitment to this course is a waste of our time and yours."

I sit forward, rubbing my pants nervously, as I bare my soul to the man. "You should know that I have no interest in collaring anyone, Master Nosh."

He frowns. "Why is that?"

I sit back in the chair, feeling uncomfortably vulnerable. "If you are familiar with my history, then you understand why."

"I know of the tragic circumstances surrounding your father's death."

I flinch as images of blood and my father's lifeless eyes flash in my mind. I clear my throat, struggling to regain my composure. "I signed up for the Dominant Training course to learn from the best of the best, Master Nosh. That is the only reason I am here."

He nods, accepting my answer. Glancing at the portrait on the wall, he states quietly, "Perhaps, in the future, we can talk about the lessons I've learned from Little Wolf."

"I look forward to it."

I leave his office feeling both relieved and confused. On one hand, I'm grateful the trainers trusted my abilities enough that they felt comfortable pairing me with Headmaster Kennedy's daughter, but I feel as if something bigger is going on.

Alana begins the evening by referencing a previous lesson. "I spoke to you about the term sub-drop. That many submissives experience an emotional or physical low after enjoying an intense scene, which is why aftercare is so important."

She smiles and asks the class, "Have you ever heard of the term Dom-drop?"

Slater snickers.

Alana raises an eyebrow, giving him a hard stare. "Only a fool would laugh."

Slater immediately wipes the grin off his face and apologizes to her.

Alana leans against her desk. "Dom-drop is something rarely talked about, but it can happen to any Dominant after a scene. Unless you understand that it is completely normal, it can take you by surprise, leaving you unprepared when it happens."

Pushing away from her desk, Alana walks around the room. "Imagine riding the powerful high of a well-executed scene and then suddenly crashing when the endorphins wear off. That crash can leave you feeling unusually irritable, tired, or mentally exhausted."

She says with a note of sympathy, "But that is not the only hurdle you face as a Dominant. We often enjoy activities that society tells us are wrong or perverted. For some of you, that may trigger feelings of depression.

She returns to lean against her desk. "Then there are the perfectionists. Because they are responsible for the wellbeing of their sub, they are often overly brutal with themselves when something fails to go as planned."

"Guess what?" Alana pauses, before stating in a gentle tone, "We are only human."

She begins walking the room again. "I have found there are times when aftercare is as much for my benefit as it is for my submissives. The simple act of holding your sub is soothing, and caring for them after an intense scene can help to strengthen your bond and open deeper lines of communication between you."

She looks directly at me when she adds, "Being a successful Dominant is not about being perfect, it's about being honest with yourself and knowing your limits."

Her statement challenges me.

I've always embraced my high standards regarding everything I do. In fact, I consider it one of my greatest strengths. It motivated me to succeed against all odds when I was a young boy. Without it, I don't know if I would have been able to survive the fallout of my father's suicide.

For me, perfection is the goal. Anything less is failure.

Unlike the weekday classes, Saturday is structured differently. Instead of a formal class with Alana, it begins with an extended practicum involving all of the experts we have worked with during the week. This allows each of us to seek out additional one-on-one instruction in the areas that interest us the most.

I appreciate that the Dominant Training curriculum's main focus is to introduce us to as many different techniques and tools as possible, but that it still allows each person the chance to further their skills in particular areas.

There's only one problem—I can't choose only one. I want to be an expert in them all!

So, I move from expert to expert during the extended practicum, seeking to pick up on the most important techniques for them all. Naturally, that does not go unnoticed by the trainers.

Laird walks up while I'm watching Kat practice swinging a vampire paddle under Madame Dubois's watchful eye. The esteemed Domme traveled from France for the week specifically to work with us because she believes so strongly in the program.

Laird throws his arm around my shoulder and says in amusement, "Watching you is like watching a honey bee going from flower to flower."

I chuckle self-consciously as I look at the five experts scattered throughout the large, dungeon-style classroom. "To be honest, I don't want to miss any of this."

"I can appreciate that. The talent represented here tonight is remarkable."

"It is," I state wholeheartedly. "But I suppose you're here to encourage me to focus on only one?"

He slaps me on the back. "Not at all, Mr. Davis. I admire your tenacity. Feel free to soak in as much as you can."

I do exactly that, peppering each talented Dominant with every question I can think of. By the end of the session, my mind is buzzing with the knowledge I have gained.

And, just when I thought it couldn't get any better, they surprise us by ending the evening with a formal demonstration of wax play by an expert in the art, Domina Avery.

Until her instruction, I thought of wax candles as purely sensation play. However, Domina Avery opens my eyes to the beauty of wax through the artistic way she uses the colors to create stunning works of art by using the human body as a canvas. She even shares the edgier side of wax play by utilizing a knife while removing the wax.

It takes the seemingly gentle sensation play to a completely new level.

Our evening ends with the six of us pairing up to practice on one another. Kat finally gives in to Ravenson's request to choose him as a partner but checks in with me first.

"Are you okay with me switching partners?"

"Of course," I assure her, adding with a smirk, "I'm looking forward to coating Ashford Ashford in wax."

I find it humorous that the moment Ashford hears that Ravenson is dropping him as a partner, he immediately pairs up with Lofton. Which only leaves me with Slater…

Surfer Boy shakes his head violently. "No way in hell am I working with you!"

"I feel the same," I answer, shrugging. "And, yet, here we are."

Vendari Steele walks up to both of us. "Is there a problem, gentlemen?"

"I cannot work with this man!" Slater states.

"Are you unable or unwilling?

"I flat out refuse," he answers, glowering at me.

"This is part of the curriculum, Mr. Slater," Vendari Steele replies. "Unless you are unable to perform the assignment, you are expected to participate."

"And, if I don't?" Slater challenges the trainer.

"Then you will have made your choice and must leave."

"What? You're kicking me out of the program?"

"No, but an unwillingness to complete this assignment demonstrates a lack of commitment on your part."

"You've seen this guy!" Slater protests. "Every chance he gets, he's in my face, trying to cause trouble."

"Exactly what has he done, Mr. Slater? Be specific."

Surfer Boy glowers at me. "He purposely slammed into me during the violet wand demonstration. And you wouldn't believe the lurid things he's said about Alana. Then there was last night!" He points to me. "The asshole almost knocked a trainer out with the door after accosting me in the bathroom."

I grit my teeth as I listen to the man accusing me of all the very things he has done.

However, it turns out that the trainers are not so easily manipulated.

"Why haven't you reported the issue?" Vendari Steele demands.

"I didn't want to make waves."

"And now?" Master Nosh interjects, stepping up to us.

Slater glances at the Head Trainer nervously. "Look, he's the problem here, not me."

Master Nosh turns to face me, frowning. "What do you have to say, Mr. Davis?"

I look Master Nosh in the eyes when I tell him, "I am not the instigator in the situation. Even so, I have no issue working with Slater tonight."

The Head Trainer turns to Surfer Boy. "Without proof or an admission of guilt, our hands are tied, Mr. Slater. Therefore, the decision remains yours. You may choose to continue or walk out of these doors."

Slater's face turns beet red while the entire class stares at him, waiting for his decision.

"Fine!" he finally shouts, shaking his fist at me. "If you try anything…"

Master Nosh growls. "Physical violence is never acceptable."

Slater looks at him sheepishly.

I force myself to keep a straight face. At the same time, I'm loving every second of it when I say, "Tell me what your hard limits are with wax candles and I will honor them."

His face screws up in frustration when he realizes he's made himself look like a fool.

Master Nosh puts his hand on Slater's shoulder. "Let me alleviate any concerns you might have." He then gestures to the other trainers. "We will all be watching you both to ensure nothing happens."

I watch Slater's Adam's apple bounce up and down as he swallows hard. With no other option but to go through with it or quit, he suddenly rips off his shirt and growls, "Let's get this over with…"

Scening with another Dominant who is unwilling is an odd challenge, to say the least. But Slater's open hostility is no match to my amusement as I coat his skin in the colorful wax.

To entertain myself, I keep checking in to ask if he needs to call his safeword.

Slater is not amused, which entertains me more.

Despite my reluctant subject, by the conclusion of the session, I feel confident in my skill with wax. Although Slater would only allow me to use his back as my canvas, I was able to quickly discern that the "art" aspect of wax play is not my forte. I'm far more interested in the sensation play of hot wax—both applying it to the skin and removing it.

My preferred method of removal turns out to be a knife, although the flogger is interesting because of the visual display it provides when the pieces of wax fly off the skin.

Being more curious than Slater, I ask him to use the different candles on display so I can note the heat levels based on the types of wax he pours on my back. Then, after coating the rest of my skin with baby oil to avoid the wax sticking to any hair, I ask him to drip the hot wax on my chest and thighs.

I take note of the areas I find particularly sensitive to the heated wax and plan to experiment further with the submissive the trainers assign me during our next practicum.

Slater flat out refuses to remove the wax from my chest and thighs, stating he's uncomfortable with the man-to-man contact. I find it a comical excuse since he's been partnered with Lofton before this.

However, I take his dissent in stride and use the knife to peel off the pieces of wax one chunk at a time from my own skin, gaining even more insight into the process.

At the end of class, Master Nosh asks the two of us to remain. As Kat passes by me, she whispers, "I'll be waiting outside."

Slater looks at me with contempt. I know he's jealous of my friendship with Kat, but he's a fool. Surfer Boy has made it obvious that he sees Kat as a conquest, not a fellow Dominant. He appears to be blind to the fact that she is only interested in camaraderie as an equal.

While I stand there, Master Nosh takes Slater to the side to speak privately with him for a few minutes. The Head Trainer then instructs him to remain where he is and walks over to me.

"Is there anything you would like to say concerning Mr. Slater?"

I'm completely honest with him. "I have no idea why Slater is intent on pushing my buttons, but I've chosen not to react. My energy and focus are solely on this course."

"So, you have no issues with him to note?"

"None worth mentioning."

Master Nosh nods in satisfaction and commands, "Shake hands and let that be the end to this tomfoolery."

Slater lets out a frustrated sigh but dutifully walks over and holds out his hand to me. When I take it, Master Nosh states quietly, "You can never understand the actions of another until you understand their history."

We both stare at him.

I'm uncertain which one of us Master Nosh is referring to.

Buddy

On the way to my car, I find Kat standing in the parking lot waiting for me. I notice the others are hovering nearby, probably hoping to find out what Master Nosh had to say.

Kat smiles as I walk up. "Hey, since it's still early, you want to hang out at the local pub?"

Ashford immediately joins us, inviting himself. "Sounds good to me."

"I'm in," Lofton states.

Amused, I glance at Ravenson. "Are you coming?"

He shrugs. "Why not?"

"I'll drive if you like," I offer to Kat.

"Great." Kat smiles, opens my car door, and slips in the back with Ravenson.

Ashford claims the passenger seat without even asking. I shake my head, finding it ironic since he chose not to partner with me in class.

I look up to see Slater staring straight at me. "Feel free to meet us at the pub. Lofton still needs a ride."

Slater feigns disinterest, but mutters to Lofton, "I'll drive you in an actual car, not that fucking rust bucket."

I roll my eyes. For all Slater's trash talk, I'm the one with the car full of people. As we head out, I spot a small shop with a collection of candles in their window display.

"I need to make a quick stop," I announce, parking on the curb. I don't have any candles for Monday's practicum, and with Anderson arriving tomorrow, I won't have time to buy them.

Hurrying into the shop, I ask the owner to point me to the soy candles. Since it'll be my first wax play with a submissive, I want to start with low-temperature candles.

I can tell the shop owner is proud of her selection when she points out her large assortment of soy candles but urges me to buy her favorite candles made of beeswax. Knowing beeswax burns way too hot, I quickly pick four soy candles—red, purple, blue, and yellow.

After complimenting my color choice, she asks, "These are lovely, but wouldn't you rather have all of the same color rather than four different colors?"

I grin. "I am a man who likes variety."

She smiles and nods. Placing the candles in a white paper bag with the shop's name and logo printed in red, she carefully stuffs red tissue paper between each candle to cushion them. Handing the bag to me, she says kindly, "Enjoy, sir."

I smirk on hearing the woman unknowingly call me by my title. I'm certain this little shopkeeper has no idea how much these candles will be enjoyed by my submissive.

Heading back to the car, I set the bag down at Ashford's feet. When we pull up to the pub, I see Slater leaning against a red Dodge Viper. His arms are crossed and he is staring at me with a superior look on his face.

"Now, that's a hot car!" Kat exclaims. "Too bad the owner's such a tool."

Laughter spills from my vehicle as I pull up beside the hot rod.

Ashford opens the passenger door. Unfortunately, the bag in the footwell falls to the ground as he makes his way out of my vehicle. Slater immediately swoops down to pick it up and opens the bag.

"What do we have here?"

"Give it to me," I demand, not amused.

Surfer Boy riffles through the tissue paper and holds up each candle, laughing. "I sure hope these aren't for me."

"They're not," I growl in irritation, snatching the bag from him and placing it back in my car.

Slater bumps shoulders with Ashford, telling him, "You better watch yourself around that guy. He's way too touchy-feely for my comfort. Tried to get me to touch his thighs in the name of 'research'…if you know what I mean."

Seriously?

I'm questioning why I invited the guy to join us.

Opening the door of the pub for Kat, she gives me a knowing look as she passes by. "Don't let the tool get under your skin."

I smile, chuckling to cover my irritation.

Once inside, however, the casual atmosphere of the pub and the friendliness of the bartender quickly loosens all of us up. Before long, I'm laughing with the rest of them as we talk about the challenges we've faced this first week.

To my surprise, it turns out that Slater is excellent at impersonating people. He has the entire group in stitches mimicking each of the trainers. Then he turns to me with a glint in his eye.

Copying my voice, he says, "Hello, I'm Thane Davis. Don't bother bowing at my feet. I know I'm above you all even though I drive a junker and can only afford apples to eat."

His voice impersonation is spot on, and I find his jab at my favorite snack actually funny. I join in their laughter but stop the moment I spot chastity entering the pub.

She waves, smiling at the bartender enthusiastically.

Then she notices me, and that beautiful smile grows even wider as she heads in my direction.

I immediately hear Master Nosh's warning play in my head. *You are not allowed to fraternize with any of the submissives you've worked with during training…*

Wanting to respect the rules of the institution, and not willing to risk expulsion, I quickly pull out my wallet and hand Kat a couple of twenties. "I hate to do this, but you'll have to take a cab back to the school. I'm heading out."

The timing couldn't be worse when it feels like we are finally starting to gel as a group. However, I know I must leave. I don't want them to find out who chastity is and why I can't be seen with her.

Without saying another word, I turn away and start

toward the back of the bar.

"Don't be like that, Davis! Can't you take a fucking joke?" Slater complains behind me.

Escaping out the exit, I head to my car. I can hear their laughter from outside and wish I could rejoin them. But, as I pull out of the parking lot, I realize it's all probably for the best. I still need to run a few errands before Anderson's visit.

I shake my head in disbelief that he's coming tomorrow. I don't normally leave things until the last minute.

But the fact is, I haven't had any time to prepare and I'm picking my friend up tomorrow.

Early the next morning, I head to the busy airport, wanting to meet Anderson at the gate. I spot him walking off the jetway decked out in his cowboy hat and boots, escorting an old woman. He doesn't even notice me as he walks past.

"Anderson," I call out.

He turns and breaks out in a grin. "Hey, buddy! It's good to see you."

Anderson turns to the lady. "Mrs. Lieberman, let me introduce you. This is Thane. He's the friend I've been talking about."

The old woman looks up at me with a twinkle in her eye. "Brad tells me you're a Master of the Arts."

I smirk, amused by his description of me. "It's a pleasure to meet you, Mrs. Lieberman."

"You are such a fine-looking gentleman," she gushes. She looks at Anderson and then adds, "You both are."

"Honeypot…mind introducing me to your two boyfriends?"

I turn to see an older man dressed in shorts and a Hawaiian shirt walking up. Anderson immediately holds out his hand to him. "You must be Mr. Lieberman. I recognize you from all of her pictures."

"Aren't they such handsome boys?" Mrs. Lieberman giggles sweetly, giving her husband a quick peck on the cheek. "But, not quite as handsome as you, dear."

The man winks at his wife. "Just keep telling yourself that, honeypot."

Anderson tips his hat to her. "Until we meet again, lovely lady."

Leaving Mrs. Lieberman blushing, Anderson claps me on the back. Together, we start down the terminal. "Mighty kind of you to meet me at the gate."

"Of course." I glance at him as we walk. The guy is tanner and more muscular than the last time I saw him. "Country life seems to agree with you."

He raises a critical eyebrow as he looks me up and down. "It's definitely a lot healthier than pushing papers from dawn to dusk."

Despite recently spending a whole day with Durov on the beach, the slight tan I had disappeared within days and now, sadly, I have nothing to show for it.

He elbows me good-naturedly. "You're almost as pasty white as you were in college."

"I resemble that remark." I snort and tell him, "That's why we're headed to the beach. I hope you brought a swimsuit."

He lowers the waistband of his jeans, showing off his neon trunks. "As soon as we hit that beach, I'm throwing off these clothes and diving into those clear blue waters."

I chuckle as I lower the waistband of my gray sweats. "Great minds think alike."

Anderson grins, slapping me on the back again. "Can't tell you how much I've missed you, buddy."

I didn't realize until now how much I missed having him around. Once we collect his luggage from the baggage carousel, we head to my car. "I wanted to invite Durov to join us at the beach today," I share, "but he's up in San Francisco for a couple of weeks staying with friends in an area called 'Little Russia'."

"Little Russia, huh? I bet he's living it up, then."

I nod, smiling. "It certainly sounded like it when I called."

When we reach the car, Anderson pats her on the roof, murmuring, "Hey there, old girl" before getting in.

He'll never know how much I appreciate that simple gesture.

"Motivation's air conditioning doesn't cool like it used to," I warn him as I start the engine.

He chuckles. "I like that you named your car. I believe every trusty steed deserves a name, whether they're made of flesh or metal. We call my pop's Chevy truck Old Faithful. He bought her in 1968, and she has been with our family ever since—even through tornadoes, blizzards, and hailstorms. You know what?" he asks, smiling at me. "After all these years, she still starts right up."

I like that Anderson comes from a humble background and understands.

As we sit in traffic, waiting to leave the airport, I remind him, "If you get too hot, you can roll down your window."

He gazes out of the window, smiling. "You *do* realize I ride horses with the sun beating down on me, and they don't come with air conditioning, either."

I laugh, thinking how different our lives are. I can't imagine living like a cowboy, but a part of me envies Anderson. Out here in LA, life moves fast—sometimes too fast. If you can't keep up, you'll be left in the dust.

Anderson lets out an audible sigh when he finally sees the ocean. "Damn, I miss this."

"I do, too," I admit. "I never seem to make it to the beach unless I'm with you or Durov. How pathetic is that?"

"Pretty damn pathetic," he agrees.

Getting out of the car, I vow, "I'm going to have a house on the beach someday. That way, no matter how busy I get, I can always come home to this…" I gesture to the beach, listening to the soothing sound of the ocean waves rolling in.

"Your own little piece of heaven."

"Exactly." I grab a cooler out of the trunk of my car and hand it to him before grabbing the rest of the beach paraphernalia I've packed. "Mark my words, Anderson. I'm going to make it happen."

"Oh, I have no doubt, buddy. I know how tenacious you are."

I stop for a moment, moved by his confidence in me. I've discovered that surrounding yourself with people who believe in you is life changing.

I had that when I was a kid. But, after a seemingly idyllic childhood, I was left unprepared for my father's suicide and my mother's subsequent abandonment.

Watching Papa' die in my arms when I was fifteen completely shattered my world, but it was my mother's betrayal that forever damaged me. Her malignant words are still buried in the darkest depths of my soul—*like a cancer.*

They lie there inside me. Waiting…

Having lived in survival mode ever since, I keep my eyes focused on the future, and have worked hard to drown out the past.

It's why having friends like Anderson are vital to me. He reminds me that *I* control my destiny—not the desperate act of my father or the demons I inherited from my mother.

I stake out a place in the sand and lay out my beach towel before stripping off my clothes. Anderson is right there beside me as we race to the water.

Using powerful strokes, I widen the gap between us, wanting to swim past the breaking waves. Once there, I float on my back in the water while I look up at the blue sky.

I feel like I am the only soul on the ocean as I stare up at the vast sky while the ocean swells gently rock me. It is both humbling and empowering.

That is…until Anderson bursts out of the water like a flying fish. He purposely lands on top of me, sending me deep into the depths. A natural swimmer, I easily escape his clutches and break the surface of the water, laughing.

"I may not ride a horse, but I know how to ride a wave, big guy."

I notice a large wave rising behind me and I start swimming toward the shore to catch it before Anderson can dunk me again. I swim even faster as the wave picks me up and carries me far away from him. I look back at Anderson and throw up my arm in victory.

Having too much fun, the two of us end up bodysurfing for hours. Finally exhausted, we head back to the beach, and I lie down on the warm sand. Letting out a satisfied sigh, I tell him, "I haven't felt this relaxed in a long time."

"The last time I felt this relaxed was after a session with a cowgirl who couldn't get enough of my bullwhip."

I chuckle. "Nice."

Reaching for the cooler, I pull out two thermoses and hand one to him.

"What's this?" He grins, screws off the top, and tilts the thermos back.

"You might want to—"

Anderson sputters and starts choking, quickly swiping his mouth. He holds up the thermos, staring at it with a look of admiration. "Is that what I think it is?"

I smile. "Yeah…it's not made for chugging."

"Damn it, man," he says, licking the drips rolling down the thermos. "You should have warned me."

"I tried!"

Anderson clinks his thermos against mine, a grateful

smile on his face. "This sure does bring back memories."

"It does," I agree as I take a sip, enjoying the unique, smoky flavor of the smooth, high-end whiskey. I think back to the day we first met in our dorm room and Anderson shared his grandfather's whiskey with me.

"We were just snot-nosed kids back then…" Anderson states before taking a long, appreciative sip.

I snort. "You realize it wasn't that long ago."

He looks at me with those intense green eyes. "You and I were different people back then, buddy. It feels like a lifetime ago."

I nod slowly, realizing he's right. Raising my thermos in a toast, I tell him, "Here's to surviving and making it to the other side."

"In one piece," he adds before taking another sip.

I deeply admire the guy because I know how fucking hard Anderson had to work in college, getting a double major while working after school. It was especially hard for him when all he wanted out of college that first day was to party and find the right "shoe" for his large asset.

"Here's to finding that elusive shoe," I tell him, clunking my thermos against his.

"I'm totally okay with searching a bit longer, buddy. No need to rush." He grins devilishly, downing another sip.

"So, what are your plans now, Anderson?"

"After Pop gets this business deal secured with the grocery chain, I'm heading to Denver to find a nine-to-five job and an old Victorian fixer-upper. As much as I love Morning Wood Ranch, I'd prefer having a steady income and weekends off."

I look at him in surprise. "Do you have any experience renovating houses?"

He places his hand over his heart, chuckling. "Nope. But I've always had a soft spot for old houses, and I love a good challenge."

I laugh, taking another drink. "More power to you, friend."

"What about you, buddy?"

"I'm working hard to advance my career. Knowing the kind of business I want to build, I'm evaluating what works and what doesn't work at this company."

"Do your bosses know you plan to eventually leave?"

"My plan is to do such a superior job improving their labor and operational efficiency that I have multiple companies competing with offers." I hold up my thermos again, grinning. "What better way to create a superior business of my own than to work for the best companies out there?"

"Genius," he says, nodding in approval.

The whiskey is definitely having the desired effect. I feel relaxed and happy—a rare state for me.

"So, are you interested in any of the submissives you've met at the Center?" he asks as he lies back on his beach towel.

"Funny you should ask." I chuckle with amusement. "I'm actually not allowed to fraternize with any of them until the course is complete."

He frowns. "Why's that?"

"They don't want us to get distracted."

"Sounds like Catholic school to m—" Anderson stops mid-sentence and sits up, his eyes glued on a woman in a tiny pink bikini walking past.

"I do miss seeing bikinis…" he mutters.

The woman looks similar to someone he and I met at this very beach. "Do you remember Rhythm?"

He nods. "I was just about to ask you the same thing, buddy." Swiping his hair back, Anderson smiles. "Do you remember how much she liked chocolate sauce?"

I nod. "Best picnic lunch ever."

Anderson sighs pleasantly. "I can't believe that was my first threesome."

"Mine, too," I state as fond memories of the encounter play in my mind.

Anderson suddenly elbows me. "Hey, I think we are being watched."

I glance over and see a shapely woman with a wide-brimmed hat smiling at us farther down the beach. When I meet her gaze, she waves for us to join her.

Anderson throws on his cowboy hat before waving back, muttering under his breath, "Do you think she likes chocolate sauce?"

Three-way Tie

"**M**a'am," Anderson says respectfully, tipping his hat before joining the woman on her towel. I sit down beside her and notice she lowers her eyes momentarily in response to my proximity. It is a subconscious sign of respect.

"I know this seems awful forward of me, but when I saw you two men walking on the beach…" She turns to Anderson. "…you in your sexy black hat…" She then turns to me. "…and you in those gray sweatpants. Well, you both had my attention."

The woman's emerald eyes light up when she adds, "Then I watched you strip down to your swim trunks and I saw the rest of you…" She wipes a tear from her eye. "Pure perfection."

Anderson immediately accepts her compliment with his easy charm, "Anything to please a lady."

"Consider me very pleased," she announces, holding out her hand in greeting. "Mister…?"

"Anderson," he answers, raising her hand to his lips.

"But you can call me Brad, darlin'."

"Oh, my! You just made me swoon."

Turning her attention to me, she bites her lip teasingly and confesses, "I want you to know I've never done anything like this before. I just…" She lowers her eyes again. "I've spent my whole life playing it safe. But I'm fifty-five now."

She looks up to meet my gaze again. "Today's my birthday, actually. And I made myself a promise not to spend another minute holding back and wondering what I've missed."

I raise an eyebrow. "And what have you missed?"

A pleasant blush colors her cheeks. "Well, for starters, I'm wearing a bikini today. I haven't worn one since I was a teenager. But, I thought why not? You only live once, right?"

I glance appreciatively at the flattering coral color of her bikini which contrasts beautifully with her tan. The outfit accentuates her impressive cleavage and curvy figure. "An excellent decision."

"I second that," Anderson adds.

"What else have you missed?" I ask encouragingly.

She glances down again. "I came to the beach by myself today because all of my friends canceled on me. Normally, I would have just stayed home…" She glances up again, her eyes flashing with spirited defiance, "…but this is my birthday, dang it!"

"Happy birthday, little lady," Anderson murmurs seductively.

She blushes. "Aww…thank you, Brad."

She is all smiles when she turns to me, then she suddenly looks bereft. "How rude of me! I haven't even asked your name yet."

"You can call me Sir Davis."

She raises her eyebrows. "Sir Davis? Oh, I like that…makes you sound all royal or something."

I chuckle, enjoying her childlike openness. "And your name is?"

"Vivian. Vivian Rose."

"Vivian Rose," I repeat in a low voice, appreciating the way it rolls off my tongue.

"Hearing you say my name like that just gave me goosebumps, Sir Davis."

I can feel the sexual tension between us building.

Her eyes sparkle when she gushes, "You two have made my day perfect by agreeing to sit with me here on the beach."

"Is there anything we could do to make your birthday *extra* special?" Anderson asks.

"I…" she stammers nervously, "I'm afraid to ask."

"No need to be afraid," I assure her, lifting her chin with my finger to gaze into her eyes.

Vivian nods. Taking a deep breath, she confesses shyly, "I've always wanted to be spanked by two men." She adds with a trembling whisper, "Naked."

I look at her intently. "That can be arranged."

Her eyes widen and she squeaks, "Really?"

Anderson moves in closer, tipping his hat. "It would be an honor to spank the birthday girl."

The pure joy on her face is extremely satisfying.

Vivian suddenly begins gathering her things, mumbling distractedly, "My place isn't too far away…"

I reach out and hold her still, insisting, "Let us pack your things."

Anderson winks. "You *are* the birthday girl, after all."

Vivian's place is unusual because she lives with two other renters in the same house. What makes it different is that each renter lives in a particular section of the old house, and they each have their own private entryway. Vivian's section happens to be the attic, and we walk up a long flight of stairs attached to the side of the house to get to her door.

I listen to her keys rattle as she unlocks the door and opens it wide with a flourish. "Ta-da!"

Stepping inside first, I notice the apartment is very small and the walls slant inward to form the roof of the attic. I can understand why she chose this place when I look out the large window and see the clear view of the ocean above the rooftops.

Her queen-size bed, covered in a floral comforter with a multitude of decorative pillows, is the focal point of the small space.

She glances at it, blushing.

"Would you like something to drink? I can offer you diet coke or orange juice."

I hold up the thermos in my hand, which is still half-full. "I brought whiskey."

"Would you like to mix it with the coke?"

Anderson shakes his head, taking the thermos from

me. "No, darlin'. I plan to drink it directly off your skin."

Her eyes widen and she giggles nervously.

"Of course, if you'd prefer to stick to a simple birthday spanking, we are happy to oblige," I assure her.

She looks at both of us excitedly. "No, I love the idea! But, if you are serious about licking me, then I'm taking a quick shower."

"We're quite serious, Miss Vivian," Anderson answers.

A little squeak escapes her lips as she runs to a tiny bathroom in the corner of the room and shuts the door. She immediately opens it again, begging, "Please don't leave while I'm gone."

Her concern is charming.

"No need to worry. We'll be making ourselves comfortable while we wait," I promise.

She makes that little squeak again before closing the door. Seconds later, we hear the shower turn on.

Anderson claps me on the shoulder. "Feels like old times, buddy."

I stare out the large window and smile. "It sure does."

"How should we proceed?" Anderson asks me as he begins to undress.

"We'll let her direct this encounter," I reply, ripping off my t-shirt before removing my sweats.

By the time she opens the bathroom door, she finds us both lying on her bed, completely naked.

Vivian walks out of the bathroom, wrapped in a towel. She stares at us as if she can't believe what she is seeing. Putting both hands to her mouth, she cries excitedly, "This can't be really happening!"

I hold out my hand to her. "Come to bed."

She walks toward me as though she is being irresistibly drawn to me. I watch her eyes widen when she notices Anderson's substantial girth. Her gaze then darts to my cock, and she unconsciously licks her lips.

Still wearing his hat, Anderson asks with a drawl, "Ready for your spanking, birthday girl?"

"Oh, God, yes!"

"You can lose the towel, darlin'."

Vivian doesn't move, but she does say hesitantly, "To be honest, it's been a while since I let a man see me naked."

I understand her insecurity, but there is no need for it. "Bare yourself."

She immediately responds to my command and opens her towel, letting it fall to the floor.

I smile while Anderson lets out a long whistle of appreciation.

Vivian is a curvaceous piece of art. Her large breasts and wide hips are more enticing than she knows, so I tell her, "Turn and show us all of you."

Biting her bottom lip, Vivian turns slowly, letting us enjoy the roundness of her belly and the plumpness of her lovely ass.

I long to plunder it all and command, "Come."

Without needing further urging, Vivian jumps onto the bed and crawls in between us, lying on her stomach.

Trembling in anticipation, she looks at us both.

"Shall we take turns spanking her?" I ask Anderson as we sit up and get into position.

"Definitely."

"Do you like it hard or soft, Vivian?" I ask before we begin.

"Medium, Sir Davis," she answers with an excited squeak.

"Medium it is, then."

I hold up my hand and call out the number one as I spank her soundly on the ass. The sight of her flesh rippling so tantalizingly from the impact captivates me. Vivian lets out a sweet little yelp, followed by a string of giggles.

Anderson counts out her second swat, filling the air with a satisfying smack.

I rub her ass cheek lightly before I deliver her third spank.

The two of us take our time, using her birthday spanking as a form of sensual foreplay.

By the time we are done, my hand is tingling and her ass is a beautiful shade of hot pink.

She wiggles her ass playfully, asking, "Now that you've got me all warmed up, what are we going to do?"

I reply in a seductive tone, "That's up to you, Vivian."

She grins up at me. "What would you like?"

I smile to myself. I suspected, based on her subtle reactions to me, that she was a natural submissive. However, in this vanilla situation, I will not be pushing her boundaries. Instead, I give her options.

"The two of us can satisfy you orally, or we can take turns penetrating your irresistible pussy. Or, if you prefer, we can even claim that sweet ass of yours."

"Can I pick all three?" she giggles.

"Of course you can…" I answer, leaning in for a kiss as I reach down between her legs to feel how wet she is.

She whimpers excitedly when I touch her pussy.

Anderson reaches over to the nightstand and grabs the thermos. "While my friend eats your pussy, I'm going to lick this whiskey off your gorgeous breasts."

Moving positions, I settle down between Vivian's legs and look up to see her watching Anderson. He tilts the thermos above her left breast and lets the liquid drizzle slowly onto her skin.

Her nipple instantly hardens as the whiskey rolls down her breast. Anderson laps up the liquid and then leaves a trail of kisses as he moves in for her nipple.

Vivian moans in pleasure when his mouth encases her nipple and he begins to suck.

I stare at her pussy in appreciation, drawn to the enticing outer folds that resemble the petals of a pink flower. However, her succulent clit has me captivated. Grazing it lightly with my fingers, I hear her moans deepen.

Spreading her outer lips, I take the first lick. Vivian's taste is earthy and sweet, and I take another, longer lick savoring her excitement.

I love the fact that every pussy tastes different—that a woman's essence is solely unique to her. It makes the experience of connecting with a woman using all five of my senses that much more exciting.

I lose myself in the sound of Vivian's amorous cries as I tease and caress her clit with my tongue. When I feel her thighs tighten around my head, I know I am having the desired effect.

I've learned to stay consistent whenever that happens. The moment a woman responds favorably, I know it's my cue to continue exactly what I'm doing with the same force and speed so she can ride out that sensual feeling to its fullest.

I find the clit a mysterious and charming part of every woman. It begs to be played with, but it can also be shy and elusive. I enjoy the challenge of that, and my passion is to find the sweet spot that will send my partner into sexual nirvana.

"Yes, yes, yes!" Vivian whimpers, clutching my head with her hands.

Keeping the same pace and pressure with my tongue, I tease her swollen clit, certain she's close.

Anderson can hear it, too.

I detect the smoky scent of the whiskey as he splashes more on her breasts. The combination of my tongue teasing her pussy and Anderson licking and sucking her breasts eventually sends Vivian over the edge.

She lets out a long, glorious cry of release as her pussy pulses against my mouth as she climaxes.

I groan in excitement, turned on by her release. After her orgasm ends, I spread her legs wide and stared hungrily at her wet pussy. "I need to dive inside you."

"Oh, hell yes!"

I reposition Vivian so her head is near the edge of the bed, and Anderson stands beside her, his hard shaft just inches from her lips.

"Don't be afraid, darlin'. I aim to please."

She turns her head and looks up at his massive cock,

murmuring hungrily, "I'm not afraid."

I press my cock against her opening as I watch Vivian take his large shaft in her mouth. She is an eager lover, grasping him tight with both of her hands, trying to take his cock down her throat.

Impressed by her enthusiasm, I'm careful to penetrate her pussy slowly so she won't choke on his shaft.

I want Vivian to have complete control as she enjoys pleasuring his cock.

So, rather than thrust into her forcefully, I take my time, concentrating my efforts on rubbing the head of my shaft against her swollen G-spot. Having already come once, it doesn't take long before her thighs start trembling.

Vivian pulls away from Anderson's shaft momentarily, looking at me in disbelief. "It feels like I'm going to come again."

"Good…" I murmur huskily.

"You don't understand. I've never come more than once. I can't."

With my cock wedged deep inside her, I stroke her wet pussy with my fingers. "Vivian, you are going to come many times."

I smile as I start back up, stroking her even deeper with my cock.

She throws her head back and cries in a joyful voice, "Oh, my God, that feels so good."

I tease her clit with my fingers while I continue to stroke her with my cock, creating a sensual friction against her G-spot.

Vivian goes back to eating Anderson's cock but soon

stops when her thighs begin shaking again. I grasp her wide hips and ram my cock into her, enjoying the view as I thrust into her repeatedly.

"I'm coming!" she cries in triumph. A pink blush peppers her chest as she comes around my cock, her whole body shaking from the intensity of it.

Afterward, she looks up at Anderson in disbelief. "I just came again."

"I know." He grins. "Now that you're primed and ready, would you like this cowboy to claim your pussy, too?"

She stares at his massive shaft for several seconds before stating with confidence, "Yes, I would, Brad."

Anderson glances at me. Since his girth intimidates most women, this is an unexpected gift.

I lie beside Vivian on the bed and start playing with her nipples, knowing it will help her body to relax.

While I please and tease them, Anderson positions himself and asks, "Ready?"

She nods, her eyes transfixed on his shaft as he starts thrusting his hips slowly. She gasps when the head of his cock enters her. I wrap my lips around one nipple and start sucking while I pinch and tug the other nipple with my fingers.

Vivian moans loudly, enjoying the dual stimulation, and opens her legs wider. Because of his immense size, it takes a long time for her body to adjust to his girth.

It allows me the luxury of exploring the rest of her body with my hands. When I turn Vivian's head to kiss her on the lips, she kisses me back—with abandon.

"Yes, Vivian, I want to feel your desire," I whisper in

her ear before kissing her again.

She growls in response, grasping the back of my neck and kissing me deeper.

The woman is on fire, drawing us both in with the intensity of her desire. It isn't long before her thighs begin trembling again.

"Oh, no…" she whimpers.

"Let it happen, Vivian."

Anderson stops when her entire body stiffens. Seconds later, her hips start bucking, drawing his shaft deeper inside her.

By the time her climax is over, she has tears in her eyes. "I can't believe I just came again."

Anderson leans down, grinning. "Darlin', we're just getting started."

I reach between her legs, lightly teasing her sensitive clit while Anderson starts thrusting again. Encasing her nipple with my lips, I ride the erotic connection as she takes Anderson's solid strokes.

I count four consecutive orgasms the moment Vivian embraces the power of her femininity and opens herself up to them.

Anderson pulls out, needing a moment to quiet his libido.

Vivian lies there silently, looking at us both. I can tell she wants something but is too shy to say it.

I sweep away a lock of her hair and look deep into her eyes. "What is your one last birthday wish?"

"I've always wanted…" She stops, her bottom lip trembling.

"Yes?" I ask encouragingly.

She stares into my eyes, finally finding the courage to say her wish out loud. "I want to know what it feels like to take two men at the same time."

I kiss her on the lips. "Wish granted."

Without saying a word, Anderson tosses his hat, and it lands neatly on a nearby chair.

Vivian grabs some lubricant from her nightstand drawer and hands it to me, excitedly.

Anderson and I take our new positions. He lies on his back, helping to support Vivian as she slowly lowers herself onto his cock. Meanwhile, I open the tube of lubricant and liberally coat my cock with it.

Vivian watches me intently, her excitement palpable as she waits.

I'm deliberately slow with my actions, knowing she has waited a lifetime for this moment. I want her to remember and savor it.

Climbing onto the bed, I position myself behind her. "Vivian, tell me when I am deep enough."

She nods her head enthusiastically as she looks down at Anderson.

"Lay your chest against his," I command in a sultry voice.

Vivian slowly lowers herself, giving me free access to her ass.

Excited, I grasp both buttocks in my hands and squeeze them hungrily, appreciating the feel of them. Spreading her cheeks, I put lube on my finger and rim the sensitive area before slowly penetrating her anus to coat her inside.

I hear her moan softly in response.

Pressing my hard cock against her pink rosette, I grasp her hips and slowly guide my shaft inside her. Vivian's breaths come in increasingly rapid gasps as she experiences the painful pleasure of taking two men for the first time.

I slowly begin rocking my hips, allowing her body time to relax as my cock disappears deeper inside her, centimeter by centimeter.

"Oh. My. God," she whispers hoarsely.

"Do you want me to stop?" I ask.

"No…"

"Reach down with your hand and feel the two of us inside you."

Anderson and I both groan when her fingers brush against our cocks.

"That's so hot!" she cries.

I slowly begin thrusting again while her fingertips remain there. It turns me on, and I seriously have to hold myself back from coming.

"Deep enough," she calls out.

I stop, noting how deep I am so I can maintain that depth moving forward. "Would you like us to come inside you?"

She pants. "Yes…please."

She removes her fingers so she can brace herself against Anderson's chest. Knowing this is her first time, Anderson stops moving, his massive shaft still inside her.

I begin thrusting.

Vivian screams, "Holy fuck-a-moly!"

I find it charming, but struggle not to laugh.

Anderson and I are both on the edge. The tight constriction of her body and her passionate cries of pleasure increase my libido to a dangerous level and I know I won't last long.

But I want Vivian to experience a final orgasm, so I keep my strokes even as I fuck her shapely ass.

When I finally feel the telltale signs of her impending orgasm, I adjust my angle slightly and hear her cry out, "Oh, oh, oh…it's happening again!"

I slap her butt in satisfaction. "Come for me, birthday girl."

She screams at the top of her lungs as she climaxes. Her inner muscles pulse powerfully, squeezing our cocks as she comes.

Anderson and I climax at the same time, unable to control the urge any longer.

The apartment suddenly falls silent as the three of us lie together on the bed, panting softly.

"Oh, my God, I felt you both come inside me," Vivian murmurs with a lazy smile.

"We did, darlin'. It was a three-way tie."

"And a powerful one at that," I add, kissing her sweaty cheek.

She sighs, grinning at both of us. "I feel like a brand new woman. How is that possible at fifty-five? This is the best birthday, ever…"

Turning her head. she looks at both of us in wonder. "If I hadn't been brave enough to ask you to join me at the beach, this would never have happened."

I smile, tucking a lock of her hair behind her ear. "If you don't ask, the answer is always no."

She grins. "I'm claiming that as my new mantra."

"Excellent," I tell her, sealing it with a kiss.

Honey

After experiencing such an eventful day on the beach, it's hard to jump back into my normal routine. I slam my hand down on the alarm clock, giving myself five more minutes, but before it can go off again, I force myself up and head to the shower.

I leave my apartment, shutting the door quietly so I don't wake Anderson, who is soundly asleep on my couch. After jumping into my car, I notice the bag of candles in the backseat. I'm looking forward to my first session with wax and trust the submissive I'm partnered with will enjoy the temperature play I have planned.

Knowing I have that exciting scene to look forward to seems to make the day run more smoothly. Rather than feeling stressed like I normally do, I feel energized.

That evening, I listen intently to Alana's lesson on setting up protocols for a submissive.

"Protocols reinforce the power exchange experienced by the submissive, and they can cultivate a deeper level of intimacy between the two of you."

She explains that there are three degrees of protocol: high, formal, and casual. I'm fascinated by the various rules a Dom can set—things such as expected greetings, submissive poses, and subtle gestures while in public. Then there are more comprehensive protocols, those involving dress, daily routines, and even interaction with others.

Different protocols can be set for particular situations, such as the behavior a Dominant expects from their submissive in public, at kink events, or when the submissive is alone.

A Dominant sets their protocols based on their personal preferences, taking into consideration their submissive's individual needs. Protocols can either be a complicated set of rules or quite simple, depending on the Dom.

I note everything she lists, pondering which protocols I would insist on if I owned a sub.

Despite my interest in the subject, my thoughts start drifting to the practicum ahead and I inadvertently glance down at my tool bag and smile.

"Mr. Davis, is there something you would like to add?" Alana asks, calling me out on my inattentiveness.

Quick on my feet, I answer her with a question, "Is it possible to have too many protocols set in place?"

She appears pleased by the question and asks, "Clarify what you mean by that."

"Can a Dom set so many protocols that instead of enhancing the connection with the submissive, the protocols actually detract from it?"

"That is something to keep in mind, certainly."

Alana looks around the room. "As a Dominant, you must find a balance that works for you and your submissive. It may look different depending on the submissive or the situations you face. Always remain open to altering your protocol if the need arises. Failure to do so could prove detrimental."

I nod, appreciating her wisdom.

When the bell rings, I'm the first to stand up. On my way out the door, Ashford inadvertently bumps into me, pushing me into Slater.

Slater immediately pushes me back, snarling, "What the hell? I thought we were done with this crap."

I hold my hands up. "Look, it was unintentional. Ashford collided with me."

Lofton, acting as Slater's minion, inserts himself between us, looking as if he's prepared to take a swing at me.

"What's going on here, gentlemen?" Alana asks sternly as she steps out of the classroom.

I look around distractedly, suddenly realizing I've dropped my tool bag and can't find it anywhere.

"I wasn't doing a damn thing to him," Slater growls in answer.

"Is that right, Mr. Davis?" Alana asks me.

I look her in the eye. "It's nothing, Alana. Ashford bumped into me, and I bumped into Slater. That's all that happened."

Kat speaks up. "That's exactly what I saw."

I glance at Slater. "We're good, right?"

He stares at me for a moment, then nods.

"Keep it that way," Alana warns before glancing at

her watch. "You don't want to be late for the practi-cum."

I'm grateful when Ashford hands me my tool bag. "Thanks."

He grunts in response, then starts down the hallway with the rest of the group. Slater glances back at me with a scowl on his face. It seems as if he and I are back to square one.

I enter the new room set up for our practicum and am impressed with the different styles of binding tables. As always, the panel of trainers sits waiting for us.

"Good evening," Master Nosh begins. "We trust you have taken the time to plan out a wax scene that will not only please your submissive but be entertaining for her as well. For this session, we want you to incorporate a protocol for the scene as well."

I snort, challenged by the requirement. I know the protocol I choose to set needs to be something beneficial to both the Dominant and the submissive, but I don't know with whom I'll be scening or what her needs are. It makes it a difficult assignment.

"You may set up your scene while we wait for the submissives," Laird tells us.

I start heading to a leather bondage table, but Slater beats me to it and gives me a smug look as he starts laying out his candles.

I then spot an intriguing red table with a cage built underneath. I consider it far better and quickly claim it. I set out my candles and the knife I have brought to remove the wax. I then ask permission to leave the room to get some ice.

Maestro Leo gives his approval.

Returning with a covered bowl, I set it on the stand next to the candles. Tonight, my sub will get to experience hot wax on her skin and the unexpected chill of ice. I cannot wait to see the expression on her face when I surprise her.

I stand beside my table and wait patiently. I notice Ashford standing nearby. His eyes are fixed on the door, and he looks as anxious as I am for the submissives to arrive.

I have come to associate the unique sound of heels clicking down the hallway with pleasurable anticipation.

I watch as the new collection of submissives enters the room, but then I catch my breath when I see a woman who looks eerily like my mother. The sight of her sends chills running down my back.

I glance away to reign in my composure. It takes me a moment, but I am able to push back the memories that threaten to rush in.

I don't need this—not now.

Ashford gives me a strange look.

I shake my head and focus my attention on the submissive standing closest to me. She's a petite redhead in pigtails wearing a short skirt and thigh-high socks. I notice her stealing covert glances at the bondage tables.

Master Nosh is aware of it, too. "Honey."

She immediately turns her attention to the floor. "Yes, Master Nosh?"

"I will see you immediately following the practicum."

The girl sounds heartbroken when she answers. "Yes, Master Nosh. I'm sorry."

"We will talk about it later."

She bows her head respectfully.

Addressing all of the submissives, the Head Trainer commands, "Join your Dominant for the evening."

The submissives bow to the panel of trainers before turning to us. My heart starts to beat wildly as the woman who resembles my mother heads toward me. I never mentioned anything about her or her appearance in my application, but I now know it is an absolute hard limit for me.

I let out an internal sigh of relief when she walks over to Ashford.

"Good evening, Sir Davis."

I look down to see the redhead smiling up at me. She immediately bows at my feet. "I am honored to serve you tonight."

With gratitude, I place my hand on her head. "Stand and serve me."

I am mesmerized by the girl's bright green eyes. She immediately lowers them, blushing. "Forgive me, Sir Davis. I have a curious nature and it gets me in trouble sometimes."

"How so?" I ask, amused.

"I have to look at everything. The moment I walked into this room, I wanted to take it all in. And I couldn't resist looking into my new master's eyes even though you had not given me permission."

I know it is standard for the submissives at the Center to keep their eyes lowered in class situations such as this, but it is not something I personally care about. Lifting her chin, I tell her, "The protocol for our scene is that you should keep your eyes on me the entire time."

She nods enthusiastically.

I add with a smirk, "And, whenever you come, you are to say, 'Thank you, Sir.'"

She grins. "It would be my pleasure, Sir Davis."

I graze her freckled cheek with my thumb. "You will call me Sir tonight."

She bats her eyes when she answers, "Yes, Sir."

"I'll be using candles that burn at a low temperature tonight, but if you get uncomfortable at any point, use the word 'yellow,' and if you want me to stop, call out 'red.'"

"I enjoy wax play, Sir. I am sure it won't be necessary."

I nod and ask her, "Do you have any limits?"

"No, Sir. Use my body as your canvas."

"Oh, I will, honey."

She smiles, a blush rising to her cheeks.

"Are you interested in intercourse afterward?"

She looks me up and down lustfully. "That is my favorite kind of aftercare, Sir."

"Perfect." Folding my arms, I look her over with approval. "The schoolgirl outfit is charming. However, for this scene, you must strip completely."

"Would you like me to strip now, Sir?"

"I would," I answer in a seductive tone.

Honey keeps her green eyes on me as she slowly unbuttons her blouse, showing off a lacy white bra underneath. Slipping off the thin blouse, she then kicks off her shoes and slowly unzips her skirt, letting it fall to the floor. She is the picture of perfection with her matching white lace panty set and those white thigh-high socks.

Leaning against the red bondage bench, she rolls down each sock and slips it off. Honey bites her bottom lip as she reaches behind her back and unhooks her bra. With a glint in her eye as she looks at me, she slips the straps from her shoulders and lets the bra flutter to the ground.

Her breasts are petite and her nipples a light shade of pink against her creamy white skin. Shimmying out of her lace panties, she shows off her nearly bare pussy with its thin patch of red. That little strip of red is incredibly enticing, and I lick my lips.

Holding out my hand, I guide her to the table and lift her onto it. "I assume you like to be bound?"

"Only with those I trust."

I raise an eyebrow. "Do you trust me?"

She nods confidently. "I can read people, Sir. Your countenance screams trust."

I smirk, both amused and honored by her declaration. "Then bound you shall be."

Before I begin, I hold up each candle so she can see the color before I light it.

"Those colors are going to look beautiful on my skin," she purrs.

"I was thinking the same thing," I agree hungrily.

Taking my time, I bind her wrists and ankles with the red cuffs attached to the table. Glancing over to see if the candles are ready, I notice Ashford's partner out of the corner of my eye. She's bound to his table as well but positioned on all fours. The woman arches her back as he pours the hot wax down between her shoulder blades. My stomach turns, still troubled by her resemblance to my mother.

Turning away from them both, I refocus my attention on the beautiful submissive bound to my table. "Which color should we start with?"

"Purple. I love the color purple!"

I pick up the pillar candle, which now has a nice pool of melted wax in the center. Hovering over her stomach, I slowly tilt it.

The moment the wax lands on her skin she let out a scream. Goosebumps rise on my skin as I react to the sound and quickly wipe the wax away with my hand, listening to her cry, "Red, red, red…!" over and over again.

I am shocked by how incredibly hot the wax is.

In an instant, Vendari Steele is by my side, handing me a cold compress. I place it against her skin to cool the burn.

"Honey, I'm sorry," I murmur and quickly undo her bindings. "I don't know what happened."

She sits up, looking up at me tearfully, her bottom lip trembling as she struggles not to cry.

I am completely devasted by what I have done.

A few minutes later, a medic arrives at the table. He lifts off the cold compress, and I am forced to confront the damage I've caused. Her pristine skin is now marred by an angry red mark where the wax made contact with her skin, and I can already see blisters forming.

Tears prick my eyes as I take her hand and squeeze it. "They were new candles. I should have tested them on myself first. I'm sorry."

"It's okay, Sir," she answers in a quavering voice.

The medic helps her off the table and walks her out of the room. The silence that follows is deafening as all eyes turn to me.

Master Nosh stands beside Vendari Steele and asks me, "What happened here?"

I shake my head, looking down at the candles. "I bought soy candles because of the low melting point."

Master Nosh picks one up and frowns. "These do not feel like soy wax."

"I honestly thought they were soy candles, but I must have picked up the wrong ones at the shop." Looking down at the floor, I frown, realizing my error. "I should have tested them before I used them. This is my fault."

"Yes, it is," Master Nosh agrees. "Thankfully, you removed the wax quickly or she might have suffered permanent scars."

I shudder, horrified by the thought.

Vendari Steele addresses the entire group, "Mistakes happen. It is a risk we take when we choose to play out a BDSM scene. Even the simplest tool can cause permanent damage if you are not careful, as was evidenced tonight. It happens to all of us at some point, but it is our duty as a Dominant to learn from those mistakes and ensure they do not happen again."

His words sound muffled and far off.

The only thing I can hear are her screams, and the only thing I see is the look of pain on her beautiful face.

I broke the trust she placed in me. I was responsible

for her care and wellbeing, and I failed her.

Master Nosh grabs my shoulder, interrupting my thoughts. "Go to my office and wait for me there, Mr. Davis."

I nod absently, heading to the door.

Master Nosh calls out to the rest of the class, "Continue."

I hear the activity in the room start up again as I leave. But, instead of heading to Master Nosh's office, I head straight to my car.

I have no business being a Dominant. The mistake I made was inexcusable and there's no coming back from this.

I unlock the door to my apartment and find Anderson dancing in the kitchen with his headphones on while whipping up a dish.

I try to sneak into my bedroom without him noticing me, but I hear an inhuman screech and then he starts laughing. "You scared the crap out of me, buddy. I thought you had class tonight."

The minute I turn around to face him, he frowns. "What happened?"

"I don't want to talk about it."

Anderson immediately turns off the stove and leaves the kitchen. He grabs me by the arm and guides me to the sofa. "You look like you just got hit by a Mack truck."

"It was a Mack truck of my own making," I tell him miserably.

"What do you mean?"

I swallow hard, finding it difficult to say the words out loud. "I hurt my submissive tonight."

The ugly admission hangs in the air like a curse on my soul.

"How?" he asks in disbelief.

The ill-fated scene replays in my mind as I voice my failure out loud. "I burned her skin with the candle because I failed to buy the right kind."

Anderson shakes his head. "I don't believe it. I know you, buddy. You're anal about that kind of thing."

I shrug, frustrated and disheartened by the whole evening. "Apparently, I wasn't careful enough, and that poor girl paid the price for my mistake. I not only destroyed her trust, but I may have ruined her love of wax."

I bury my head in my hands, ravaged with guilt.

Anderson wraps a brotherly arm around me. "Thane, I've made mistakes with the bullwhip. There have been several times when I cut skin when I only meant to cause welts. It happens, buddy."

"Your mistakes involved skill, Anderson. My mistake was so fundamental that there can be no excuse for it."

Anderson snorts. "If I remember right, you wanted to take this course to become a better Dominant, right? Well, it's better to make that mistake under the watchful eyes of experts than to have it happen when you're alone."

I groan. "I can't even imagine what the trainers think

of me now. But whatever they think doesn't compare to what I think of myself."

Disgusted and embarrassed by my failure, I tell him, "I'm done."

"Done taking the course?"

"No. All of it."

Anderson stands up, declaring, "You can't quit! That's the dumbest thing I've ever heard."

I look at him, trying to adequately express how I feel. "Honey trusted me. I'll never gain that trust back because I destroyed it with my incompetence." I close my eyes. "I will never forget the look of fear and pain on her face."

Sighing miserably, I mutter, "I caused her harm when all I wanted was to please her…"

He smacks the back of his hand against his palm. "There is a huge difference between breaking someone's trust on purpose and breaking it by making a mistake. A *huge* difference!"

I shake my head. "In the end, my intentions have no bearing on the situation. The only thing that matters is knowing that a young woman is suffering tonight because of me."

Anderson starts pacing the small apartment. "You're not thinking straight right now, buddy."

Feeling defeated, I stand up and head to my bedroom.

"I've got an idea!" he shouts behind me.

"I don't want to hear it," I snarl, shutting the door behind me. I strip off my clothes and lie down on the bed, crossing my arms over my eyes.

The day started with such promise and ended in ashes.

My phone rings, and I glance over to see it's Master Nosh. I have nothing to say to the Head Trainer. I once held such promise, but that ended today.

I'm a disappointment to him—and myself.

Unable to sleep, I toss and turn, reliving the scene over and over again.

Eventually, I hear a woman's voice outside my room and freeze. Glancing at the digital clock, I see it's one in the morning. I have no idea what Anderson is up to, but I want no part of it.

Throwing on my sweatpants, I storm out of my bedroom and immediately stop in my tracks.

I stare at her, my jaw slack.

Anderson claps the woman on the back and smiles at me. "Well, look who's here."

Compassion

"Hey, Thane."

I'm unprepared for this encounter and look at Anderson questioningly.

"I knew there was only one person who could talk some sense into you," he informs me.

Samantha looks at me apologetically. "If you don't want me here, I'll leave."

I shake my head, but I have no idea what to say to her and the two of us stand looking at each other in awkward silence.

"Let me get you some drinks!" Anderson announces, heading to my small kitchen.

I gesture to the sofa and watch as she sits down, her long blonde hair flowing as she moves with cat-like grace and the unmistakable confidence of a Domme.

"It's been a while," I state, still in shock that she's here.

Samantha looks up at me with a sad smile. "It's been like almost six months, I think."

I snort in disbelief. "Crazy how fast time passes."

Anderson comes waltzing back and hands us two glasses. "Whiskey on the rocks."

Samantha frowns, handing it back to him. "I don't drink anymore."

"Damn! I forgot. Sorry about that." He quickly snatches the glass away from her.

"No reason to be sorry, Brad," she assures him. "However, I would like some water."

"Of course. Let me get you that." He looks at us both excitedly. "You guys keep talking."

I watch Anderson leave to fetch the glass of water and ask, "How are you, Samantha?"

She purses her lips, then nods silently as if pondering the question. "I'm actually doing surprisingly well."

"Really?" I did not expect that kind of answer from her.

Her red lips curl into a genuine smile. "Yeah. It's taken a long time and a lot of hard work, but things are finally settling into place."

I smile, genuinely pleased. "I'm glad to hear it."

She looks at me pensively. "How is Durov?"

I sigh, downing the entirety of my drink before I answer. The topic is a complicated one for me, and difficult to articulate. I was the one who introduce Samantha to BDSM and I brought her and Durov together. Their chemistry was off the charts right from the start, but there was also tension between them because they were both Dominants.

I'm certain Samantha still loves Durov, despite what she did the night she assaulted him while intoxicated. By trying to force Durov to submit to her physically, she destroyed their relationship and caused him permanent psychological scars.

Durov suffered in silence for months after the incident but eventually cracked. After flying into a blind rage at a frat party, he came close to killing Samantha with his bare hands. No longer able to trust himself around her, he left the States to return to Russia.

Before he left, however, Durov made me vow to watch over her. He knew she had fallen into a deep depression and was dangerously close to ending her own life, and he asked me to support her through it.

I found myself in the ungodly middle of their drama. My loyalty remained with Durov, but I felt responsible for Samantha—and her mistake.

I had actively encouraged her to explore BDSM, and shared what I was learning with her. She'd been a good friend to me in college and stood by my side when my unhinged mother attacked me. Samantha even risked her own life when my beast of a mother threatened me with a gun. I feel indebted to her for that.

Setting my glass down, I tell Samantha, "Durov is well." When I see her face light up, I add, "But I refuse to answer any further questions about him. He is not your concern. You need to let him go."

She looks at me sadly but nods.

Anderson returns with her water. "I'm glad you could come here on such short notice, Samantha."

I turn to him, "Why did you invite her?"

He looks at me with compassion. "You need to talk to Samantha about what happened tonight."

I frown as a flood of guilt washes over me. "I specifically told you I didn't want to talk about it."

"Trust me, buddy, it needs to be addressed right now," Anderson insists. "I know you too well."

Samantha says with concern, "What is he talking about, Thane?"

I close my eyes and wish I could disappear. But the warmth of the alcohol flowing in my veins lowers my inhibitions, and I find myself detailing what happened. I start at the awkward moment when I saw my mother's lookalike and tell her the rest up to the final moment after the wax burned my submissive's skin.

Samantha looks at me with sympathy I do not deserve.

When I finish my story, Anderson adds, "He wants to quit."

"You can't do that!" Samantha exclaims.

"There's no excuse for the mistake I made. If I could hurt someone with a fucking candle, what right do I have to call myself a Dom?"

Samantha reaches out and touches my hand. "I know you don't want to hear this, but you should look at it as a gift."

"Gift?" I snarl. "What an asinine thing to say!"

Samantha doesn't flinch at my anger—or my words. "I need you to hear me out, Thane."

I glare at Anderson, not wanting any part of this.

He just smiles while he fills my glass with more whiskey.

"Making a serious mistake early on as a Dominant will serve you well in the future," she insists.

I shake my head, feeling as if I'm being coddled when I deserve zero sympathy from her—or anyone. I have no patience for it.

"Listen to me," she demands.

I grit my teeth as I wait for her to speak.

"The memories of seeing her in pain will never leave you."

I unconsciously grimace, knowing what she is saying is true.

"But those memories will keep you alert, Thane. You will never face a scene the same way again because you know the damage you can cause."

Samantha looks deep into my eyes. "You should be grateful it was a mistake that had no lasting effects. Based on what you said, you reacted quickly, and she was given immediate medical care."

"Still, I betrayed her trust."

Pain clouds Samantha's eyes when she says, "No, Thane. What I did to Durov was a betrayal of trust. You simply failed to check the temperature of the wax."

"But I knew better."

"You *did* know better, but you were in a new environment with a new sub, and you were thrown by seeing a doppelganger of your mother. You are only human. Humans make mistakes all the time."

I frown, unable to reconcile my failure.

"I know you," she states with conviction. "You will never allow yourself to make the same mistake again, regardless of the type of scene it is. Because of the pain you caused, you will be vigilant about testing all of your equipment. But it encompasses even more than that.

You will see every aspect of the scene with new eyes and be a better Dom because of it."

I shake my head.

"Yes, Thane. I know this because I've lived it. I failed as a Dominant in the vilest way a person can. But the ugly truth is, even though I thought of myself as a Dominant, I wasn't one—not even close. I didn't realize it at the time, but I never put my submissive's needs ahead of my own. I was playing at being a Dominant, and I relished having my needs fulfilled. It wasn't until I came to care more about my submissive than myself that I stopped being a danger to us both."

Her words are profound.

Tears fill Samantha's eyes. "After assaulting Durov, I wanted to die. But, with the professional guidance of my psychologist, I was able to dissect what happened that evening and the reasons behind it. Rather than wallow in my guilt, I made positive changes to guarantee it never happened again.

"I stopped drinking, joined AA, and sought out the mentorship of the highly respected Domme Mistress Blaze. I served under her as a submissive until I fully understood both sides of the power exchange."

She looks at both Anderson and me. "Because of what happened, and my actions afterward, I can say with confidence that I am a good Domme now. I'm not saying that out of pride but with humility. My heart is in a place to serve my submissives well even as I demand the best from them. Not only that, I'm committed to the learning process and to growing as a Dominant for the rest of my life."

"That's good to hear, Samantha," Anderson says. "I admit there was a time I hated you after what you did to Durov."

She nods. "You were right to."

Samantha turns to me and grabs my hand. "You are not me. You have always been a Dominant, Thane. You care about your submissives and want what's best for them. That has never been a question."

After a restless night, I head to work but I feel hollow inside. Although I appreciate Samantha's insight, I can't stop replaying the scene with honey over and over again in my mind.

The experience has rocked me to my core.

When my cell phone rings shortly after arriving at work, I glance at it and groan. It's Master Nosh. Although I would prefer to avoid speaking to him at all costs, I dutifully answer the call.

"Why did you leave last night when I specifically told you to wait in my office?"

I'm completely honest with him even though it hurts me to say it. "There is no point in me continuing."

Master Nosh doesn't even argue the point. "I expect to see you in my office at noon."

I huff. "That's impossible. I'm at work."

"I am certain you can figure it out. Do not disappoint me again."

His words cut like a knife. I deeply respect the man

not only as a Dominant but also as a person. Knowing I've failed him too adds to the disgust I feel with myself.

After hanging up, I head to my boss's office and ask for an extended lunch. I cringe a little, knowing I recently ask for the day off when Durov showed up at the office.

He looks at me thoughtfully. "Is everything okay?"

"I'm fine. This is simply a matter that needs to be addressed today."

He nods. "Well, you've always stayed late when I've asked. I'll grant it."

"Thank you, sir."

I leave work early, anxious to get this meeting with Nosh over with. The one thing I hate more than failing is having someone rake me over the coals for it.

However, I know I completely deserve it in this situation.

As always, Rachael Dunningham greets me with a pleasant smile. "Lovely to see you, Mr. Davis. Master Nosh is waiting for you in his office."

I linger at her desk for a moment, feeling the need to tell her, "You are an asset to this institution, Miss Dunningham."

She blushes. "Why, thank you. That is so kind of you to say."

"Simply the truth."

I walk away, fully expecting not to return to the Center after this meeting with Master Nosh. Deciding to face my fears with courage, I knock on his office door.

The Head Trainer answers it himself and, without speaking, gestures for me to come inside. I walk into the office and sit down, waiting in silence as he takes his place behind his desk.

"Explain to me why you left last night."

Rather than make excuses, I tell him the truth. "A sub was hurt last night because I failed to check the temperature of the wax. The mistake is inexcusable, and I cannot forgive myself for the oversight. Therefore, I have decided to quit the program."

"Why would you do that?" he asks in a grave tone.

I frown, surprised by the question. "I hurt a person under my care with the simplest of instruments. It's obvious I cannot be trusted."

"A good Dominant owns and accepts responsibilities for his mistakes."

"I do accept it, which is why I must step down."

Master Nosh furrows his brows. "You are not accepting responsibility. You are running away from it."

His words provoke my anger. "You're wrong! I'm protecting submissives I might inadvertently harm in the future."

"What about your submissive last night? Honey is still in need of your care."

I violently disagree and remind him, "I broke her trust last night because of sheer carelessness on my part. The last thing she needs is me."

"Mr. Davis, it is obvious to me that your drive to be a perfectionist is more important to you than the well-being of your sub."

I stand up in protest and shout, "No! I'm willing to walk away from something I am passionate about because I realize I am not fit to be a Dominant."

"That is pure arrogance on your part. Your duty right now is to heal the damage you've caused. Honey needs you to accept responsibility and help guide her."

I look at him in disbelief. "I broke her trust, Master Nosh. Why in the hell would she want anything to do with me?"

"Because she gave you the gift of her submission and trust. Do not dishonor her by discarding those gifts so lightly."

I sit back down, challenged by his words. The Head Trainer is right about one thing. This entire time I have been so focused on my failure that I've failed to think how I could help honey.

I lower my head in shame.

"What you do after this is completely up to you, Mr. Davis. But your submissive deserves your time and energy right now."

I nod. "I see that now, but I am at a loss as to how to proceed from here. The last thing I want to do is cause her any more harm."

"Honey has asked to scene with you again. You will honor her wish."

I stare at him in disbelief. "I'm shocked she wants to."

Master Nosh sits back in his chair. "It is important to speak to your submissive after a scene ends badly. It is the reason I asked you to go to my office—so that the two of you could talk."

I groan, suddenly realizing how selfish I've been. When my submissive needed me the most, I disappeared on her…

I meet Master Nosh's stern gaze. "You're right. I was not thinking of my duty as a Dominant. I need to rectify the situation as soon as possible."

"Good. Honey is waiting for you right now."

"Now?"

"The sooner you rectify your mistakes, the better."

My heart begins to race as he reaches into a drawer of his desk and hands me a set of three candles. "These candles burn at a low temperature."

I stare at them, condemning myself once again for purchasing the wrong candles. "I hope you won't be offended when I test each one," I tell him.

"I would expect no less. I have one more piece of advice for you, Mr. Davis." His next words hit me out of left field.

"The compassion you feel toward others should also be directed toward yourself."

The idea is a foreign concept to me.

I stand up and nod to him, feeling both surprised and grateful for the opportunity to scene with honey again.

I *need* to make up for the harm I caused.

"Master Nosh, I appreciate your correction in this matter. I did not act in honey's best interests, but I will take care of that now."

"Use the time wisely, Mr. Davis."

I pick up the candles and head first to the Center's kitchen area to get the bowl of ice. I have every intention of playing out this scene as originally planned.

Honey deserves no less.

Trust

I enter the private room and find honey waiting for me, along with the trainer, Maestro Leo. The room has a single bondage table in the center, several cabinets, and a plethora of tools on the wall.

Maestro Leo nods to me.

Honey's head is bowed, so I place my finger under her chin and lift her head to look into those green eyes. "How are you?"

She smiles slightly. "Better, Sir Davis."

"I'm sorry about what happened last night. Not only for my mistake with the wax but for leaving before we had a chance to talk."

"I understand you were upset, Sir."

Guilt washes over me. "I was upset because I hurt you. It was the last thing I wanted to do."

She looks at me tenderly. "I know."

"Can I see it?" I ask her.

Honey lifts up her shirt to show me the dressing covering the wound. I stop her when she goes to take the tape and gauze off.

"Does it hurt?"

"Only a little, Sir. Like a bad sunburn."

I suspect that she may be underplaying the level of pain, but I do not question her on it. "Master Nosh informed me that you would still like to play out the scene."

Her smile grows. "Yes, please. I've been looking forward to it."

"Any changes you would like to add?"

"No, Sir. I trust you."

Trust.

I did not expect to hear that word from her after last night, and I am deeply moved by it.

Running my fingers down her forearm, I look my little redheaded sub over. She is wearing a new schoolgirl outfit in shades of pink. While I'm admiring her new outfit, I start to reformulate my original scene based on the injury.

Instead of waxing her stomach, I will use her back as my canvas. However, I know that laying her on her stomach may hurt because of the wound. Turning to Maestro Leo, I ask, "Can I use any item I find?"

He nods solemnly.

I leave her for a moment to check out the numerous cabinets. Searching through them, I find a white throw made of fake fur. "This should do nicely."

Maestro Leo looks at me with a smirk. "The candle wax will be impossible to clean up."

"I'll replace it then," I inform him, confident in my choice.

After I lay the soft fur on the table, I wink at honey. "I want you to have a luxurious experience today."

Unlike last night, I have decided to undress her myself. I start by unbuttoning her blouse. Lightly caressing her shoulders, I slip off her top and set it on the floor. I cup her small breasts, enjoying the friction of her lacy pink bra and the hardness of her nipples against my palms.

Kissing her tenderly on the lips, I reach around and undo it next. That too joins the blouse on the floor. I slowly unzip her skirt and then quickly free her of it. Leaning in close, I leave a trail of kisses from her throat to her chest before kneeling down. Cupping her ass with both hands, I kiss her pussy through the material of her lace panties.

She lets out an excited gasp.

Looking up, I remind her, "Eyes on me during the entire scene."

She grins. "Yes, Sir."

With that, I inch down her panties to expose her exquisite pussy with the red strip of pubic hair. I toss her panties to the side and lean in to kiss her mound before standing back up.

She moans softly as I claim her lips again. I want to build her state of arousal before the first drip of the wax lands on her creamy white skin.

Running my hands over her body as we kiss, I groan lustfully as I explore her mouth with my tongue. As much as I want to continue, I am quite aware of Maestro Leo standing there, waiting to assess my wax scene.

Breaking away, I sweep her small frame up in my

arms and carry her to the table. "I want you to lie down on your stomach. Let me know if it's uncomfortable."

Honey settles down on the table, laying her cheek against the soft fur, and purrs. "It feels heavenly, Sir."

"Excellent."

I light the three candles, and while we wait for them to melt, I bind her wrists and ankles. Now properly bound, I run my hand over her back and lightly spank her pretty ass.

Making sure I stay in her line of sight during the entire scene, I pick up the first candle and pour its wax onto my wrist to test the heat. As I expect, the temperature is warm but not overly hot. I test the other two candles, wanting her to know I am being thorough and that there is nothing to fear.

Wiping the dried wax from my wrist, I smile at her. "Are you ready to play?"

"I am, Sir."

Hearing no hesitation in her voice, I proceed. Picking up the red candle first, I tip it slightly and watch the drip fall from the candle and splash onto her skin. She moans softly in pleasure. I slowly drip a line of warm wax from her left shoulder blade down to the swell of her ass. She wiggles on the fur, her eyes never leaving me.

"Are you enjoying the wax?"

"Oh, yes…"

I set the candle down and pick up the yellow one next. This time, I make a horizontal crisscross line down her back.

"Yum," she purrs.

Setting it down, I pick up the green one and make a

V-shaped design by starting from the center of the small of her back and trailing the wax upward at an angle to her left shoulder. I then repeat the action, trailing the wax up to her right shoulder.

I stand back for a moment. My waxwork is definitely not artistic by any stretch of the imagination, but the smile on honey's lips lets me that I'm doing well.

But, I am not done yet.

I had originally planned to surprise her with the ice, but I change the plan now, given the unusual circumstances. Removing the lid to the bowl, I hold up an ice cube for her to see.

"I want you to close your eyes for a moment."

She closes her eyes, grinning.

I pick out an area of her back that is free of wax and ask, "Ready?"

"Yes, Sir," she answers in giddy anticipation.

I wait a moment to build her anticipation before gliding the ice over her back. I watch goosebumps rise to the surface of her skin.

"Oh!" she cries out in delight.

Putting the ice in my mouth, I let it melt while I grab another piece and trace it over her skin, teasing her sensitive neck and shoulders. I then move down her back to her thighs, and I even use it on her ticklish feet.

Once the ice has completely melted in my mouth, I lean over to kiss her.

Her eyes open wide as I plunder her mouth with my ice-cold tongue. "Isn't temperature play fun?" I murmur.

"It is," she says breathlessly.

Feeling in a more adventurous mood, I put another

piece of ice in my mouth as I move to the end of the table and climb onto it. Taking the ice from my mouth, I spread her open so I can lick her pussy.

She squeals the moment my cold tongue makes contact.

"Too much?"

"No, Sir," she grins.

I suck on the ice again, then take the piece and slowly slip it inside her. She makes a cute little squeak. My cock grows hard at the sound.

I go down on her then, licking and teasing her clit with abandon.

"Oh, my God! Oh, my God!" she cries repeatedly.

I am shocked by how quickly she comes. Pressing my tongue flat against her pussy, I feel every pulse of her climax.

As soon as it ends, she looks back at me. "Thank you, Sir."

I smile at her. "You remembered."

"Of course."

"Would you like to come again?"

"If it would please you."

"It would," I answer huskily. Grabbing another piece of ice, I get the same reaction from her when I flick my tongue against her sweet-tasting pussy.

"Thank you, Sir," she murmurs with luminous eyes after her second orgasm ends.

I climb off the table to return to the wax.

Picking up the red candle again, I decorate her ass with a scattering of dots. I follow it up with the yellow, and then the green candle…and that's when it hits me that the colors are the same ones used for safewords.

I find it humorous, and contemplate the message behind it.

Wanting to tease honey further, I dribble wax on the bottoms of her feet and listen to a string of her giggles.

Blowing out the candles, I tell her, "Now that your body is covered in wax, I must free you from it."

"I always love this part," she murmurs.

I pick up the knife and show it to her. Her eyes widen in anticipation as she watches me place the blade against her skin. I begin with her round ass. Lightly scraping the knife against her skin, I lift the soy wax easily from it.

The process is slow and requires all of my attention. However, I find it relaxing in an almost therapeutic sense as I watch the pieces fall away from her skin one by one.

By the time I'm finished with her back, honey's eyes are at half-mast, and she has a look of sheer contentment on her face.

That's when I go for her feet.

"Flex your feet and hold still," I command.

When she does, I lightly scrape the wax from the taut skin of the bottoms of her feet. The room is filled with honey's sweet laughter.

Ending the scene on that happy note, I unbind her from the table and help her to sit up. I then pull her into my arms while she giggles in my ear and squeezes me tight.

My lips find hers, and soon her laughter quiets as I kiss her more deeply. The atmosphere in the room changes as the two of us connect on a more sexual level.

The scare from last night seems to mix with the fun of the scene today, and the strange combination of emotions ignites our desire.

Our kisses are passionate while our hands eagerly explore each other freely.

I can't get enough of her body and my cock aches to possess her. "I must have you," I growl ravenously.

"Yes!" she whimpers with mutual need.

Maintaining our positions, I quickly undo my belt and unbutton my pants before unzipping them. She straddles me, forcing my cock into her wet pussy while I grab her buttocks to help her move up and down on my shaft.

I kiss her hard, reveling in the feel of her tight pussy squeezing my cock as I claim her mouth. The moment is both intimate and heated as she wraps her arms around me.

"May I play with myself, Sir?" she whispers.

"I command it," I murmur gruffly.

When I feel her hand slip between her legs, and she starts rubbing her clit vigorously, it takes me right to the edge. It isn't until I feel her inner muscles caressing my cock with her third climax that I finally allow myself to give in to my release.

I groan as a powerful orgasm rocks through me, and I press her body hard against me. Afterward, still holding honey in my arms, I feel weak but incredibly satiated.

"Thank you, Sir," she whispers, kissing my cheek.

We change positions and I spoon with her on the soft fur. I tell her how much I admire her courage in scening with me again so soon after the accident.

She smiles, letting out a contented sigh. "This isn't the first time I've been burned with wax, Sir."

I frown. "What do you mean?"

"It's happened a few times over the years."

I stare at her in shock. "Are all of your Doms idiots like me?"

She laughs, turning to face me. "None are idiots, Sir. Including you. It rarely ever happens, but when it does, they've always reacted quickly. I've never been seriously hurt."

I stroke her cheek. "The fact that it's happened to you before makes you an even braver soul to scene with me a second time."

"I wouldn't have missed this, Sir."

I nuzzle her ear. "Neither would I."

After she leaves the room and I've cleaned up, Maestro Leo walks me back to Master Nosh's office and informs me, "We will do your evaluation now."

I take a deep breath before I step into the office. Even though I feel the scene went well, I'm still acutely aware that I walked out last night and failed to communicate with my submissive after the failed scene.

Master Nosh sits at his desk with a solemn expression.

I sit down beside Maestro Leo in front of the pine desk to await my fate.

Master Nosh nods to the trainer. "I appreciate you

taking time out of your workday to address this issue."

Maestro Leo nods.

"Tell me what you observed."

Maestro Leo opens his notebook and details the scene, adding no personal commentary in his summary.

Before sharing his own thoughts, Master Nosh asks him, "Do you have anything to add about Mr. Davis's handling of the scene?"

Maestro Leo turns his head to look at me. "Despite the fiasco that took place last night, Mr. Davis showed genuine concern and empathy for his submissive. Additionally, it appeared to me that he made several adjustments to the scene as he went along."

Maestro Leo then turns back to Master Nosh, and adds, "By the way, he owes the school a new throw."

The Head Trainer stares intently at me but says nothing.

Continuing, Maestro Leo states, "Overall, I feel he listened to his submissive and was quick to make changes. And, because of that, he delivered a scene that adequately met her needs."

Master Nosh nods, then turns to speak to me. "Tell me about these changes Maestro Leo mentioned."

I rub my hands on my pants nervously as I gather my thoughts. "Obviously, I needed to avoid the burn area, so I focused my attention on her back rather than her stomach. However, I felt the padded table might be too painful, so I used the fake fur to make it more comfortable."

"You will be charged for that," he informs me.

I nod. "It was necessary for the scene. I don't regret

it."

His silence follows my statement, so I continue to detail the changes I made. "I originally planned to surprise honey with the ice in order to tease her with the extreme temperature change. However, after my failure last night, I was afraid any surprises might trigger her. So, I showed her the ice before using it. As a result, I learned she really enjoys temperature play. Knowing that, I extended that portion of the scene."

More silence follows, so I continue.

"When it came time to remove the wax, I used a knife. However, I chose not to emphasize the edge play aspect of the instrument and instead used it more as pre-aftercare."

He raises his eyebrow. "Pre-aftercare?"

"I was purposely slow when removing the wax and was gentle with the blade. I wanted her to feel relaxed and enjoy the simple connection it evoked."

He nods with understanding.

"Honey mentioned last night that coupling was her aftercare of choice, so we ended the scene that way. However, I spent a few moments afterward praising her for her bravery."

"Do you think she would feel comfortable scening with you again?" he asks me.

"I do."

Looking at Maestro Leo, he asks, "Do you agree?"

"Based on what I witnessed, yes."

"Fine." Master Nosh laces his fingers together. "Now, for the bigger issue…"

I sigh, knowing what is coming.

"Your failure to go to my office when I ordered you to was a grave mistake."

I frown, nodding in agreement. "It was. Not only was it immature on my part, but I failed to accept my responsibility for honey's care. Both are not acceptable as a student of this institution."

"You speak about failure a lot. Is that how you see life, Mr. Davis?"

I furrow my brow. "You either succeed or fail. Isn't that how it works?"

He shakes his head slowly.

Confused, I look at Maestro Leo.

Master Nosh states firmly, "Life is not a series of successes and failures, Mr. Davis. It is a classroom of experiences."

The concept feels alien to me.

He continues, "What you deem as 'failure' is actually an experience meant for you to learn from, so you can make the necessary adjustments in order to move forward."

He gives me a grave look. "Normally, I dismiss people like you, Mr. Davis—individuals that are so intent on the goal that they can see nothing else and miss countless opportunities for growth."

Master Nosh then leans forward. "However, you are different. While you are certainly goal-oriented, you do accept correction without letting it offend your ego."

Looking directly into my eyes, he states, "What concerns me more is that your hatred of failing caused you to question your fitness to be a Dominant so profoundly that you were willing to walk away without consulting the trainers in charge of you."

He leans back in his chair. "That comes from either extreme arrogance or an utter lack of confidence."

My eyes blink slowly as I stare at him. I feel numb as I struggle to accept his statement.

"I personally have no patience for arrogance," he declares sternly. "It is an affliction that cannot be fixed. But, I have never met a person with natural talent like yours who has no confidence in himself."

"I have confidence."

He raises an eyebrow. "One mistake and you were willing to walk away from it all."

Damn, his words challenge me. However, I can offer no defense.

"Based on your scene today, do you feel you are fit to be a Dom?"

"Based solely on that, yes."

"And, if you make another mistake…? Which you will," he adds with emphasis.

I feel a constriction in my chest.

He looks at me thoughtfully. "Life is a series of experiences, Mr. Davis. Each one is meant to expand our minds and help us grow on our journey."

Master Nosh folds his arms. "What life is *not* is a checklist of successes and failures. That is linear thinking and impedes growth."

I nod. "I hear what you are saying, Master Nosh. But it's contrary to everything I know."

"Here's what *I* know, based on what I've seen" he replies. "You clearly understand that the submissive holds equal power in the dynamic, and you are comfortable with that. So comfortable, in fact, that you accept your role as alpha and are adept at directing scenes that incorporate the mutually set parameters to the benefit of yourself and your sub. That is the key to a successful D/s dynamic."

I have no words, humbled by his statement.

"The Center has two choices, Mr. Davis. We can accept your wish to leave training based on your actions last night. Or we can offer you a second chance, with the expectation that you will move forward with confidence—*not* a fear of failure."

I look at them both, surprised they are giving me this second chance.

"I would like to stay."

"Fine. Then we will see you this evening."

I stand up and leave his office, completely stunned.

Breathless

I can't let it go.

I pass the little candle shop every day on my way to class, and every day, it reminds me of my mistake and I inwardly shudder.

Even though I have no use for more candles, I decide to return to the shop, unable to reconcile how I could have made such a grievous error.

The woman behind the counter lights up when she sees me. "Are you here for another set of candles, young man?"

I smile. "Do you mind pointing me to the soy candles again?"

This time she walks out from behind the counter and takes me to them herself. They are exactly where I expected them to be.

"Let me show you my beeswax candles," she insists. "They have the same pretty colors but are made from one hundred percent beeswax. Not only are they good for the environment, but they burn brighter and longer."

I know beeswax is not safe for wax play because its melting point is too hot, so I follow her, curious to see where she has them set up. She leads me near the window display. Sure enough, the candles look the same, but there is no way I could have mistakenly purchased them instead of the soy candles since the displays are in two separate areas.

Which leaves only one other option.

Laughing, I tell her, "The candles do look alike. Have you ever mixed them up?"

"Oh, no!" she assures me. "Beeswax is much more expensive, so I check the label on the bottom of every candle before I set them out on display, just to be sure. Plus, I always double-check when I ring them up." She giggles. "It would be disastrous for my bottom line if I didn't."

I smile at her, although her answer leaves me confused. I know I didn't pay a lot for the candles, and if she's as diligent about checking them as she claims she is, then there shouldn't have been a mix-up.

"Thank you," I tell her, starting toward the door.

"What?" she cries. "Didn't you come to buy candles?"

"Sorry, no. Not this time."

I leave the store feeling even more unsettled than before. The chances of me purchasing the wrong candles and her not catching the mistake seem highly unlikely.

I run it by Anderson when I get home.

I catch him in the kitchen, peeling potatoes over the sink. "That makes zero sense to me."

I sigh in frustration. "I don't get it."

He stops what he's doing and dries his hands. "Hey, get your candles so we can check the labels."

"I would, but I threw the fucking things away the night of the practicum."

"Well, damn, buddy!"

I growl in irritation. "I know. It was an idiot move."

Anderson walks over and pats me on the back. "You were upset. I get it."

I look him in the eyes. "Honestly, I just wanted to get rid of the evidence of my stupidity."

"You're always so rough on yourself, man. When are you going to loosen up?"

My lips twitch. It takes a moment for me to answer him honestly. "Possibly never, but I'm trying."

He puts his arm around me, laughing kindly. "Well, that's all we can ask for."

Wanting to change the subject, I ask him, "How did the meetings go this week with the grocery chain?"

He grins, slapping me on the back enthusiastically. "All I had to do was cook up several different cuts of meat for the big wigs, and you'll never guess what happened."

I chuckle. "What?"

"They ate it up! Couldn't get enough, I tell ya. Most people expect organic beef to be tough meat with less flavor, but we have a secret. We let our cows munch on fresh clover as a treat. They love it, and consumers can taste the difference."

"Huh. I have to say, I admire the care your family puts into your livestock."

"Pop is committed to giving every animal the care

and respect it deserves.'"

"So, I take it you got offered a good deal, then?"

He beams with pride. "We did, but I was able to negotiate the price even higher. I'm happy to say my double major and four years of college didn't go to waste."

I shake his hand, incredibly proud of his accomplishment. "Well done, Anderson!"

He nods, looking pleased. "It's been mighty gratifying. Of course, that means I'm heading back to Denver tomorrow to find a city job and stake my claim."

"I'm positive you'll succeed in whatever you do." I stare at him for a moment, sad that I can't celebrate his success with him tonight. "If I didn't have to go to bed immediately, I'd celebrate that contract with you."

"I've been thinking about that…"

"What?" I chuckle, wondering what he's thinking.

"You really don't have time to take care of yourself between work and this class. If I wasn't cooking for you, I don't think you'd have eaten anything all day."

I laugh off his concern. "What's a few weeks without food?"

"They call that starving, buddy."

I snort. "My body can handle it. So, what are you really getting at?"

"I have no reason to rush home now that the contract's been signed, and you could use a cook for a few weeks. What if I stayed?"

I have to admit I've enjoyed having Anderson around—even if I haven't been home much. Still, I shake my head. "I couldn't let you do that."

"Why? I'm offering."

"You shouldn't put your life on hold. Especially when you've landed the deal of the century for your family. Use that energy to find a business job you can really sink your teeth into."

He smirks. "I'm not sure if you're making fun of me or being serious."

Putting my hand on his shoulder, I tell him, "I mean it, Anderson. You need to put yourself first."

He nods and offers me a half-grin. "I thought you might say that..." With a laugh, he adds, "Always looking out for the other guy but never yourself."

I roll my eyes.

"Oh, I see that eyeroll, buddy. You may think you know it all, but you're damn stubborn when it comes to accepting help, and therein lies your weakness."

I think about it and suddenly realize the truth. "I had to look out for myself after my father died and my mother left. So, I learned at an early age that I could only depend on myself. I guess that feeling never leaves a person."

"But things have changed since then, and you need to adjust, buddy. I get why you had to live that way back then, but you have friends who support you now. Not accepting their help when it is freely offered is insulting to them and slows your progress—and I know how you like efficiency."

The low sound of my chuckle belies the fact he hit on a hard truth about me, and I don't appreciate it. "Watch yourself, Anderson."

He looks at me with genuine concern. "I just want to

help, so sue me."

I'm tempted to roll my eyes again but refrain. "I'll think about it."

He nods, but it doesn't look like he believes me.

I look at my watch and groan. "Sorry, I have to get to bed. I only have two and a half hours before I have to get back up."

"That's what I'm saying, buddy…"

Later, as I get settled in bed, Anderson raps on the door. Popping his head in for a moment, he tells me. "I just had a thought. If you didn't buy the beeswax candles, then that means someone else did. Someone who bought the exact same colors as you."

Only one name comes to mind—Slater.

I am riddled with bizarre dreams that night, and they all have a particularly specific snake theme. I have no issues with snakes, and in the dreams, I'm not afraid—until the boa constrictor.

The boa constrictor suddenly appears, along with several rattlers. The others curl up and playfully strike at each other, but the boa constrictor starts moving toward me through the grass.

I'm not afraid of it and make no attempt to run.

Instead, I watch it slither toward me at a leisurely pace for several minutes before I return to my work.

For some unfathomable reason, I'm in a prestigious cooking competition set out in an open field and there's a large neon clock hanging in midair counting down the minutes.

I already know what I want to cook, but I can't find the correct ingredients and am searching frantically in the pantry for them. I keep glancing at the clock as I check through the pantry, my anxiety rising with each minute that passes. I will have nothing to present if I don't find the damn ingredients.

I feel the huge snake brush against my leg but think nothing of it. I even nudge him away with my foot the same way a person would a dog.

I'm starting to panic during my fruitless search and start throwing ingredients left and right in desperation. I finally see my ingredients, but before I can grab them, the pantry fills up with new items.

The boa constrictor has returned, and it slowly begins to wrap itself around my legs. More concerned about losing the cooking competition than the snake, I continue with my search.

There's a feeling of doom when the clock starts chiming. It's counting down the final minute and I know I will never finish, but I—

Can't. Stop. Searching.

Meanwhile, the snake continues to leisurely wind its way up to my chest, then it engulfs my arms.

It's only when I can no longer move that I notice it is slowly squeezing the life out of me.

Suddenly, the scenes changes and everything in the field disappears except the boa constrictor.

I look up and watch the clouds float leisurely by above while I feel my lungs slowly being constricted tighter and tighter with every breath I take.

True panic sets in and I try to cry out for help, but I can't make a sound.

Cold darkness closes in around me as I lie there on the ground, dying in a field of grass on a bright summer's day.

The boa constrictor turns to look at me as it squeezes harder, stealing away my last breath even as I feel the chill of death taking over.

The creature has a human face I know well, and I let out a silent scream of terror just before I die…

I wake up and scramble out of bed, patting my chest to check if I'm okay. I can't stop gasping, trying to suck in air.

I feel like a fool. I know the snake wasn't real, but the terror I felt remains strong.

I sink to the floor and force myself to take slow, deep breaths in order to calm myself.

Before I leave for work, I quickly write Anderson a note and leave it on the counter for him to find when he wakes up.

Anderson,

After giving it some thought, I've decided you should stay. I would never want you to accuse me of being inefficient.

P.S. – Have a pot of Ribollita soup on the stove when I get home tonight.

~Thane

I shake my head at my poor attempt at humor as I head out of my apartment. The truth is, the dream has left me deeply troubled, and I'm unsure if I can face an empty apartment when I get back home tonight.

Suspicion

Work is a struggle, but I strive to keep my mind focused on my tasks and get through the day.

Although I feel certain Slater set me up knowing a submissive would be hurt, I have no proof. An allegation of this nature will have serious consequences, so I need evidence before I accuse him.

Arriving at class early, I ask Kat if she'll speak with me privately. Slater eyes me suspiciously as the two of us leave the room together.

"What's up?" she asks staring at me hard. "You look like you haven't slept a wink."

I wave off her concern. "Don't worry about me. I just want to ask about that night I bumped into Slater outside this classroom. You told Alana you saw everything that happened. What exactly did you see?"

She frowns. "Is that asshole giving you trouble again?"

"I need you to tell me exactly what you saw."

She glances upward as she thinks back on it. "If I

remember right, Ashford ran into you at the doorway, and then you collided into Slater in the hall. It was obvious Slater thought you did it on purpose because he bashed you in the chest, and his little minion, Lofton, looked like he was going to deck you."

I nod, remembering the series of events exactly as she described them. "Did you notice what happened to my tool bag during the scuffle?"

She frowns, thinking about it before shaking her head. "I don't remember anything about your bag."

Her answer is disappointing. I hoped Kat had noticed Slater messing with my bag.

Kat asks in a worried voice, "What's going on, Thane?"

Before I can answer, her eyes widen. "Oh my God, do you think Slater had something to do with what happened to your submissive?"

"It's just speculation at this point."

She snarls, "If that fucker could do something that underhanded, he needs to be kicked out of the program as soon as possible."

"I agree, but I need to find proof first."

She clasps me on the shoulder. "You want me to ask around?"

I glance down at my watch and see we only have a few minutes before class. "No, I'll take care of it. I don't want Slater getting wind of it."

She nods. "If you need my help, let me know."

I spend the class focused on Slater. I still can't wrap my head around the idea that he would purposely hurt another person to get back at me. However, I've known since the start that he wants me out of the program, and switching out my candles was certainly an effective way to do it.

Hell, it almost worked…

With my attention on Slater, I miss most of Alana's lecture on maintaining a long-distance D/s relationship. When she asks me to repeat what she just said regarding ways a Dominant can maintain authority long-distance if a sub has disobeyed a direct command, I'm unable to formulate an answer without the risk of sounding foolish.

She frowns. "I will speak to you after class."

Slater snickers under his breath.

"Mr. Slater, you will remain after class as well."

While I dislike being called out, I know it's deserved. I focus my full attention on her, spending the rest of class diligently taking notes while silently boiling inside. I resent the extent of Slater's influence in my life.

After everyone else files out, Alana calls the two of us up to her desk.

"Explain to me what is going on between you."

"Nothing!" Slater answers, pointing at me. "I have no clue what Davis's beef is now. We had things settled, but he's back at it again."

Alana looks at me sternly. "What seems to be the problem, Mr. Davis?"

Unsure of how to answer, I pause and think for a moment. "It's a private issue, Alana. I will not let it affect my performance in class again."

She looks at me with compassion. "Is it something I can help with?"

I smile, appreciating that she cares enough to ask.

Slater shakes his head in disbelief.

Alana glares at him. "Is there something you would like to say, Mr. Slater?"

He shrugs as he inches toward the door. "I'll just leave. Wouldn't want to stand between you two."

"You'll do no such thing!" she snaps. "After the session is over tonight, I expect the two of you to stay an extra hour and write up an essay on the most effective ways to build and maintain a long-distance BDSM relationship."

I can hear the ire in her voice when she adds, "Since you both wasted my time in class, you will make up for it on your own time. I expect that paper on my desk before class begins tomorrow or you both will be dismissed from the program."

"*What?*" Slater cries. "You can't be serious."

She looks him dead in the eyes without saying a word.

Her punishment is like pouring gasoline on a fire that's already out of control, and I'm left to question once again if I should even continue at the Center. However, Master Nosh offered me a second chance, and I refuse to go down without a fight.

Resisting the urge to argue, I assure her, "We'll have that paper to you tomorrow."

Slater's lips curl downward but he says nothing.

Alana hands us several books from her bookshelf,

then says dismissively, "You may leave, gentlemen."

Neither of us says a word as we make our way to the first practicum of the night. I find it difficult to walk beside a man I suspect of purposely hurting someone to get at me.

I can only hope he's sweating bullets right now because I will stop at nothing to prove his guilt.

After a riveting demonstration on fire play taught by the highly talented Mistress Blaze, a Domme I've previously met and Samantha personally worked with, I have the opportunity to feel the fiery sensation myself.

Kat and I team up to practice after her demonstration, and I get to feel the fire racing over my back for the first time. The experience leaves me flying on a euphoric high!

I have never been so interested in mastering a skill as I am tonight.

I can't wait for the first practicum tomorrow after hearing that Mistress Blaze will be overseeing it due to the dangerous nature of the medium.

The thought of being able to recreate the experience I just had for someone else is absolutely mind-blowing to me.

After such an incredible experience, I can't reconcile myself to the fact that I have to work with Slater afterward. We meet at the commons, and I immediately set the timer for one hour, unwilling to spend a second longer than needed.

It's clear Slater feels the same because he immediately takes the first book from the stack and starts skimming through it.

I shoot Anderson a quick text in case he took me up on his offer to stay longer and make dinner.

Unexpected school assignment. Will be an hour late. Talk then.

I pull out my notebook and tell Slater, "Rather than us both taking notes on the same material, how about you read out loud and I'll write it down? We'll give ourselves forty-five minutes to gather information, then consolidate it so you can dictate while I write the final piece."

"Fine by me. The sooner I'm out of here, the better." Slater starts by listing different activities a Dom can assign their sub to keep the power dynamic strong while I meticulously write each one down.

When Slater finishes with the list, he shuts the book. "You want to talk about it?"

"What?"

"Whatever's got you so riled up."

I grunt, unwilling to talk to him. "Just do the assignment."

He opens the next book and skims it for a moment before reading aloud, "'How to maintain a long-distance relationship.'"

"That sounds promising. Keep reading."

"'There is an art to maintaining any relationship, but

a long-distance one requires extra work because you rarely, if ever, see each other in the flesh…'" Slater snorts. "Isn't that rich?"

I look up from my notes. "What are you talking about?"

He laughs ruefully. "This is utter bullshit."

I put my pen down. "How would you know? Have you ever tried it?"

"Fucking lived it." Slater goes back to the book, but each word he reads only seems to agitate him more and he eventually stops again. "The person who wrote this obviously has no clue what they're talking about."

I sigh in frustration. "Your personal commentary is not helping us get the paper done."

Slater continues reading, "'Long-distance relationships aren't impossible, but they can be difficult to maintain for long periods of time.'" He rolls his eyes, smacking the book hard. "It *is* impossible. It's wrong to give people false hope."

When I realize he's not going to stop, I suggest, "Why don't you tell me why long-distant relationships are impossible?"

The depth of pain I see in his eyes comes as a shock and leaves me mute.

He looks away. "Never mind. Forget it."

I'm wondering if the endorphin high we're both experiencing after the fire play session is affecting this conversation because he's being overly emotional and I'm not as pissed at him as I should be.

"Let's get back to it," I quietly suggest.

"Fine." Slater keeps reading, "'Don't put your life on

hold for your partner…'" His voice breaks. Taking a deep breath, he continues. "'Outside of the scheduled times you have set with your partner, remember that you have a life to lead. Keep yourself busy so you aren't continually reminded that your partner is far away.'"

Slater shakes his head, looking as if he is about to lose it.

I reach over and shut the book. "Out with it."

He rolls his eyes, but I can see tears in them.

"I don't know what's wrong with me…" He lets out a breath in frustration. "Why the fuck do I care?"

I tilt my head. "Care about what?"

"That he's gone."

"Who's gone?" I frown, having no idea who or what he is talking about.

Slater growls under his breath, then mutters to himself, "Keep it together, man. Keep it together…"

I stare down at my timer and watch the seconds tick by. "Maybe if you'd say it out loud, you'd be able to move on."

The look he gives me is so painfully vulnerable that it makes me uncomfortable.

"My father died today."

The moment I hear it, my heart constricts. Memories of my own father's death spring to life. Unwanted tears suddenly prick my eyes as I struggle not to cry. Even though it's been years, it still cuts like a knife.

"You know how I found out?" Slater asks, his voice gruff.

I shake my head, forcibly swallowing down my own pain.

"The fucking newspaper. How screwed up is that? Aren't they supposed to wait until family members are told before they report shit like that? Oh, wait. That's right. I don't fucking count. Never did."

He angrily swipes at the tears that fall, growling in disgust.

I have no idea what to say to him.

Slater opens the book back up and tries to find the page he was reading.

I mutter, "Don't worry about the paper. I'll come up with something."

He glares at me. "Fuck you will, Davis. I don't trust you." Flipping through the pages at a faster pace, he eventually lands on the page.

I feel no love or comradery for the guy, but it's obvious that he is suffering. "I'm sorry for your loss."

"Don't be," he snaps, slamming his fist down on the table. "The dick stopped being a father the second he walked out the door. I was just too stupid at the time to realize it."

His statement conjures up memories of my mother. The first time I caught her cheating on my father, it severed our relationship—but I had no idea at that point.

By sheer force of will, the two of us get through the assignment and, with only seconds to spare, I finish writing out the last sentence and hand the paper to Slater to look over.

He stands up and shoves it in his back pocket.

"Wait. I just wanted you to read over the damn thing," I snarl.

"I don't give a fuck what you want. I'm keeping it

safe so you can't screw me over."

My hackles rise, and I wonder if he means that as a threat. "Give it back."

"Fuck you!" He grabs his tool bag and skips the elevator, heading straight to the stairs.

I refuse to chase after the asshole. Instead, I slowly stack the books on the table and grab my things.

Whatever it takes, I'm not letting him hurt another soul.

I return late to my apartment. I smile, able to smell the Ribollita simmering on the stove before I even unlock the door.

"About time," Anderson exclaims when I step inside. "You're lucky you asked for soup, or dinner would be ruined."

He heads to the kitchen and dishes up two bowls, asking with interest, "So, what's this about an assignment after class?"

I groan, setting down my tool bag before joining him in the small galley kitchen. "If you can believe it, I had to write a paper with Surfer Boy as a punishment for not paying attention in class tonight."

He drops one of the spoons and it clatters to the floor. "Isn't that the guy who's been messing with you?"

"Yeah. I'm sure he's the one who switched the candles, and I can't stop thinking about it."

He hands me one of the bowls and a fresh spoon.

"Did you end up ratting him out?"

Before I answer, I sip a spoonful of the hot soup. The moment I taste the Ribollita, I feel a rush of dopamine and sigh in contentment. My father used to make this dish when I was a boy, and it has become my comfort food of choice.

I hold up the bowl and smile. "Thank you. I needed this."

He grins. "Soup soothes the soul, buddy."

I nod in agreement. "As far as Surfer Boy, I didn't say anything because I need proof." I frown, thinking back on the night. "It was strange though. For a guy who is plotting my demise, he was weirdly open with me tonight."

"About what?" Anderson asks, slurping a spoonful of soup.

"He claimed his father died today and he seemed really broken up about it."

"What's the dad's name?"

I shrug. "No idea, but I assume his last name would be Slater."

Anderson looks shocked when he hears the name. "You don't mean Senator Dick Slater?"

He grabs this morning's newspaper off the counter and shows me the front page. "It's all over the news, buddy. He's a bigwig in Washington—I mean, he *was*."

I look at the photo of a middle-aged man with facial features similar to Slater's. The man is standing beside an attractive, much younger woman who's holding a Bible while the Vice President swears him in. The article identifies the woman beside him as Dick Slater's second wife.

Anderson nods at my bowl. "Eat your soup before it gets cold."

I continue to enjoy the soup while I consider the article. I feel conflicted. I understand that Slater must be reeling after his father's unexpected death, but he's still a danger to others.

I can't stand by and let another incident like what honey went through happen again.

I have to act before someone else gets hurt.

Treachery

With no snakes haunting my dreams, I'm able to get three hours of restful sleep before my alarm rings at five. I'm grateful for them. Although three hours is far from ideal, it's enough rest to get the wheels turning in my head.

As the day progresses, the pieces start to fall together. I think I have a good idea of how Slater did it and how I can prove it.

After work, I drive straight to the candle shop. The shopkeeper smiles when she sees me. "Are you here to buy candles this time?"

I chuckle. "I am."

"Which kind would you like?"

"I'm going to buy both this time—soy *and* beeswax."

"That's an excellent idea. But I bet as soon as you use the beeswax candles, you'll never go back to soy."

I smirk, knowing she wouldn't be saying that if she had any idea how I was using the candles.

I walk to the soy candle display and pick up the same

set of colors I had originally purchased. I then go to the beeswax display and do the same.

Walking up to her counter, I set all eight down.

"Those colors sure are popular," she comments, smiling as she rings up each one before packing them carefully with tissue paper in the white paper bag.

Experiencing sticker shock, I raise an eyebrow when she tells me the total.

Giggling, she reminds me, "I told you they were expensive, but I promise you won't regret it. Don't forget that they are good for the environment."

I'm casual as I segue into the main reason I'm here. "Can I ask you something?"

"Of course!" she answers, grinning as she continues to pack the candles up.

"Did a guy with a dark tan and long blond hair happen to come in here to buy candles recently?"

She shakes her head. "No, but he sure sounds dreamy."

I'm disappointed by her answer, feeling certain I'd figured it out.

"But, there was another guy…"

My heart starts to beat faster. "Can you describe him?"

"He wasn't much to look at…not like you."

I shake my head in amusement. "Can you give me more than that?"

She stops packing the candles and looks sideways, crinkling her brow. After a few seconds, she says, "I think…" She pauses, then nods vigorously. "Yeah, that's right. He wore glasses. He came in the day after you and bought the same colored candles."

Shocked, I immediately ask her, "Did he have short hair?"

"I think so, but I can't be sure. Oh, but I do remember the guy didn't say much. A kind of an odd fellow. Oh, my goodness!" She suddenly blushes, and asks, "Is he your boyfriend?"

I shake my head, ignoring her comment. "Are you sure he purchased the same four colors in beeswax?"

"Yes. I thought it was strange, but figured it must be some new decorating fad." She looks at me apologetically, her blush growing deeper. "I didn't put two and two together until now. Sorry, I didn't mean what I said about him being odd. You make a great couple."

"We're not a couple."

She grins and offers me a knowing wink. "Well, he sure must think highly of you to buy such expensive candles as a gift."

I stand there, no longer listening to the woman as I struggle with the revelation that Ashford would do such a thing. I never saw it coming…

Like the boa constrictor in my dream.

"Hello?"

I look over to see her holding the bag out to me. "If I see the young man again, do you want me to put in a good word for you?"

"Please don't," I say, wearily. Taking the bag from her, I head out of the store.

Now that I have the proof I need, I can go to the trainers about this. However, the one question I can't answer is why Ashford would do such a thing.

Walking to the reception desk, I tell Rachael, "I need to speak to Master Nosh as soon as possible."

"I'm sorry, Mr. Davis. The panel is preparing for the session tonight and cannot be disturbed."

"I understand, but this is a matter of extreme importance and cannot wait."

She smiles kindly. "I will pass the message on, but I suggest you head to class."

Hiding my frustration, I nod to her.

As I walk into the classroom, I scan the room. It feels surreal to see Ashford sitting at his desk. The guy glances up at me briefly and barely nods before turning to stare at the whiteboard. It's causal enough to count as a greeting, but there is absolutely no feeling behind it. I realize he's been that way with me the entire time.

I glance at Slater, who has a smug look on his face.

Glancing at Alana's desk, I notice our research paper isn't there. "Where is it?"

"What?"

I can't believe his level of immaturity, but I surprise him by not saying a word. Confident he is bluffing, I walk past him and sit down next to Kat. While he might want me to be kicked out of the program, I know he won't do anything that would cause him to be kicked out himself.

Sure enough, Slater waits until the last minute starts ticking down before walking up to Alana and placing the paper on her desk. She picks it up and quickly scans it. Without saying a word to either of us, she begins class as soon as the bell rings.

Slater looks at me triumphantly as if he's won.

When the push-button phone suddenly lights up on her desk, Alana finishes her sentence before picking up the receiver. "Yes?"

Her gaze immediately lands on me. "Certainly."

Hanging up the phone, she tells me, "Mr. Davis, please leave. An assistant is waiting in the hallway to escort you."

The room falls eerily silent as I pick up my tool bag and exit the room. I'm sure everyone, except for the possibility of Kat, assumes it's my walk of shame.

Slater wears a self-satisfied smirk on his face, while Ashford stares at me intently with no emotion whatsoever.

The staff member waiting for me in the hall leads me to the room where the fire play practicum will take place later tonight.

"Mr. Davis," Master Nosh calls out, standing up from behind the table.

I feel the heavy weight of all their stares as I walk up to the trainers.

Master Nosh barks, "We have little time, so speak quickly."

Nodding to him, I address all four trainers. "I believe the soy candles I purchased were purposely switched by another student before my practicum with honey began."

All four of them stare at me in shock.

"That is a very serious allegation," Master Nosh states gravely.

"I know, and I would not be coming to you if I wasn't certain."

"Who, exactly, are you accusing?" Vendari Steele

asks, in a cold voice.

"I believe Ashford purchased candles made of beeswax in the exact same colors I had, then switched our bags before the practicum began."

Laird frowns. "What reason would he have to do such a thing?"

"I honestly don't know other than wanting to discredit me."

"What proof do you have, Mr. Davis?" Master Nosh demands.

"I went to the shop where I purchased the soy candles and confirmed with the shopkeeper that a man matching his description purchased the same colored candles made of beeswax the day after I bought the soy ones."

I pull out the candles from my tool bag and lay them out. "As you can see, there is very little difference between the two sets of candles. Because the difference is so subtle, I failed to notice the switch when I was setting up my scene."

Laird seems particularly upset. "Why would Ashford put a submissive in danger?"

I shake my head, equally concerned. "I have no idea but before the practicum, he bumped into me in the hallway, and it caused a scuffle between Slater and me. At the time, I assumed it was simply an accident on his part. But, after speaking to the shopkeeper today, I now believe that is when he switched our bags."

Master Nosh calls one of the staff members and gestures for him to lean in, whispering something in his ear. The man nods and immediately leaves the room.

Maestro Leo looks unconvinced. "The plan seems far too complex."

"I don't think it was something he preplanned," I explain. "I believe Ashford saw an opportunity and took advantage of it the night he was in my car and saw me purchase the candles."

Master Nosh frowns. "Why was he in your car?"

"All of us were meeting at a bar nearby after Saturday's session, and he rode with me, along with Miss Reid and Ravenson."

"And they can confirm he was with you when you purchased the candles?" Laird asks me.

"Yes. When we arrived at the bar, Ashford accidentally knocked the bag out of my car when he exited the vehicle…" I suddenly wonder if he did it on purpose.

"Then Slater picked up the bag and showed everyone the candles."

"Slater?" Maestro Leo asks, frowning. "Do you believe he was involved, too?"

I sigh. "To be honest, I originally thought Slater switched the candles based on our previous altercations. But after speaking with the shopkeeper, I no longer believe that is the case."

"How can you be sure?" Maestro Leo insists.

"I can't. However, I have never seen the two of them interact in class."

The staff member returns and whispers in Master Nosh's ear.

"Excuse me, gentlemen. This should only take a minute," he tells the other trainers.

I stand there silently while the three remaining trainers whisper amongst themselves.

When Master Nosh returns, I can feel a wave of quiet anger pouring from him. He addresses me in a solemn voice. "Thank you, Mr. Davis. You may return to class."

"Can I ask—?"

"No, you may not."

I walk up to clear the candles off the table, but Master Nosh waves me away. "Leave them."

I quietly pick up my tool bag and walk out of the room, shaken to my core by the encounter. I have no idea what just happened, but the energy in the room feels charged like the quiet just before the storm unleashes.

When I walk back into class, everyone looks surprised to see me, including Alana. Without missing a beat, she says, "Welcome back, Mr. Davis. You may take a seat."

Kat looks at me questioningly when I sit down beside her.

I shrug and get my notebook out. I struggle to concentrate on Alana's lecture about impact play safe zones because I can feel the heat of everyone's gaze directed at me.

A male submissive walks into the classroom and begins to undress while Alana continues her lecture. Once naked, Alana orders him to stand at the front of the class, facing the whiteboard.

"It is imperative that you know the areas to avoid during any type of impact play. Hitting these parts of the body could result in extensive, sometimes fatal, injury."

She takes out a pointer and touches an area low on his back. "The kidneys must be avoided and are found between the bottom of the ribcage and the top of the buttocks." She circles the area at the bottom of his spine. "Then we have the tailbone, which is located at the base of the spine here."

Alana traces the upper part of his hip with the pointer. "You want to avoid the boney part of the hips because several nerves are located here."

Tracing down the length of the sub's spine, she tells us, "The spine in the center of the back has several small bones that can be cracked or bruised."

When she lightly grazes the base of the man's neck with the pointer, he twitches slightly. "As you can see, the neck is a sensitive area. Keep in mind that this is where many major arteries, tendons, glands, and lymph nodes are found."

Pointing to his ears, she warns, "Ears are also off limits for impact play. Hitting a person's ear may cause permanent damage to hearing—"

Master Nosh walks into the room, along with Vendari Steele, Laird, and Maestro Leo. Their unexpected presence, along with their ominous expressions, fills the room with a sense of foreboding.

Alana quickly excuses the submissive, who immediately picks up his clothes and makes a hurried exit.

"I apologize for interrupting your class, Alana," Master Nosh states gravely, "but there is an urgent matter we must address with the students."

"Of course," she replies, obviously startled by their

presence.

I glance at Ashford, who looks bemused as he stares at Slater.

Slater, on the other hand, stares at me accusingly, as if I've betrayed him.

Master Nosh addresses all of us. "It has come to our attention that a student in this classroom purposely endangered one of our submissives."

"Whatever Davis said, I had nothing to do with it, I swear!" Slater cries in his own defense.

Master Nosh turns to him. "This isn't about you, Mr. Slater."

Slater sits back in his chair, a stunned look on his face.

The other students glance at each other, obviously wondering which one of us the panel has come for. Ashford turns to me with a superior look on his face, as if he assumes I'm the one going home.

"Mr. Ashford, what do you have to say for yourself?" Master Nosh demands.

Ashford turns to the Head Trainer and calmly states, "I have nothing to say, Master Nosh. Why are you asking?"

"We have evidence that you tampered with Mr. Davis's equipment, which resulted in one of our submissives getting injured."

"You are mistaken," Ashford assures him.

"No, we are not. I have spoken to the manager at the shop where you purchased the candles before the wax play practicum. She was able to locate the receipt, which included your signature. We also have a videotape that shows the exact moment you switched tool bags in the hallway."

Ashford briefly glares at me before staring straight ahead in silence for several moments, blinking slowly.

He seems oddly unaffected by the accusation.

Then, in a flurry of motion, he bursts out of his seat and sprints toward the door.

Quick as a flash, Laird grabs and subdues him while Vendari Steele stands in front of the door, blocking his route of escape.

Master Nosh declares in a voice full of barely restrained rage, "You are not only finished here but you will be banished by the BDSM community as well."

Ashford lashes out. "You are a fucking joke. All of you are!"

He then looks directly at me.

"My IQ is far higher than yours," he says in a voice dripping with contempt. "People fawn over you like you're God's gift to women, but you are nothing—and I suspect you know that deep down inside."

He glances at the trainers and sneers. "Don't listen to their accolades, Davis, because it is given by fools."

Ashford's eyes shine with malice when he focuses his gaze back on me. "I want you to hit bottom so you can live out your truth."

Looking at Slater, he adds with a laugh, "Then there's you. Too incompetent to be of use to anyone."

"Enough!" Master Nosh snarls.

Turning to Alana, he tells her, "We are canceling class tonight. You will begin tomorrow where you left off."

Ashford fights the trainers restraining him and he unleashes a string of curses as they physically drag him out of the room.

We all look to Alana in stunned silence.

She looks particularly distraught and quietly lays her pointer on the desk. She then takes a few moments to collect herself before addressing us.

"First and foremost, our job as a Dominant is to protect submissives from harm. That is all for tonight."

As we quietly file out of the classroom, Kat comes up beside me. "I never suspected Ashford was capable of something like that."

"No one did."

I notice Slater trying to catch my attention and I tell her, "I'll see you tomorrow, Kat."

I hang back to see what the guy wants.

He shakes his head. "That was some crazy shit back there."

"I'm still in shock," I confess.

"Well, we're better off without him…" With a laugh, he adds, "Now, I just have to get rid of you."

I look up to see him cracking a smile.

I smirk. I feel a pang of sympathy for the guy knowing that his father recently died. "Want to hang out at my place for a bit?"

His eyes narrow. "Why?"

"No reason. Just thought I'd ask. Forget I said anything."

As I head out, he grumbles behind me, "If you are really *that* desperate for company, I guess I could join you…"

I roll my eyes, amused by the way he's acting as if he's doing me a favor. "Great. You can follow behind me in your car."

Before I start driving home, I text Anderson.

Class ended early, so I'm headed back. I'll tell you what went down when I get home but wanted to give you a heads up that Surfer Boy is coming too.

He immediately texts back.

Should I have my bullwhip or a whiskey waiting for him?

I chuckle when I text my answer.

Both.

Fiery Fun

When I open the door, Anderson greets us. He looks properly intimidating with his arms crossed and a scowl on his face. When I notice the bullwhip secured to his belt, I smirk.

Slater looks at him warily as he enters the apartment.

"This is my friend, Brad Anderson."

"Hey," Slater mumbles.

Anderson wraps his hand around his bullwhip and only grunts in answer.

I slap Anderson on the back. "You are not going to believe what went down tonight."

"It was fucking crazy," Slater mutters in agreement.

I tell Anderson, "I'll make a round of martinis and tell you all about it."

Slater makes a sour face.

Anderson immediately barks, "You got a problem, kid?"

"Martinis are overrated. I'm more of a whiskey man."

Anderson suddenly breaks out in a grin. "Well, now you're talking my language, Surfer."

He frowns when he hears the name. "Surfer?"

I smirk while I shake my martini. "That's my pet name for you."

"My *pet* name?" Slater snarls. "What the fuck?"

Anderson smacks him on the back. "Now, now…" He hands Slater a glass of whiskey. "Don't get your panties all in a twist."

Slater takes a drink, eyeing me indignantly.

I walk out of the kitchen, handing Anderson one of the martinis. "I made this one special just for you. It has a splash of whiskey."

Anderson flashes a smile as he takes the martini glass. "Thank you, buddy." Taking a sip, he looks surprised. "Who knew gin and whiskey would be a good combo?"

Throwing an arm around my shoulders, he says, "Now tell me all about the shitshow you've been hinting at."

"Give me a minute."

I take a long drink, appreciating the smoothness of the gin, and sigh in pleasure. "Damn, that's a good drink."

Sitting down on the couch, I set my martini glass on the coffee table and detail everything that happened, beginning with my visit to the shop. Slater adds his own sporadic commentary as I talk. He sounds as wound up over the bizarre events as I am.

When I finish, I tell Anderson, "Watching them drag Ashford out of the classroom was unreal but extremely satisfying."

Slater laughs ruefully. "I fucking thought you were trying to frame me, Davis."

I down the last of my drink and then get up to make another, telling Slater, "If we're being completely honest, I did think it was you."

He points his finger at me. "I *knew* I couldn't trust you!"

"It wasn't a matter of trust," I explain. "I based that conclusion solely on your behavior. You did insinuate that I was having relations with Alana—as well as accusing me of giving blowjobs to the panel of trainers."

"Hey, look, I was just calling it like I saw it," Slater states defensively.

Anderson narrows his eyes. "And, how do you see it now, Surf?"

Slater holds out his glass. "Set me up with another whiskey and I'll tell you."

Anderson downs the last of his martini before taking Slater's glass. While the two of us are in the kitchen, Anderson asks me, "Do you really think you can trust this guy?"

I stare at Slater, nodding slowly. "After one of the altercations I had with the guy, Master Nosh told me, 'You can never understand the actions of another until you understand their history.'"

I turn back to Anderson, "Call me curious."

He chuckles, "You *do* know curiosity killed the cat?"

Heading back with the drinks, I ask Slater, "So, how are you holding up?"

"What do you mean by that?" he snaps.

"Just a simple question. I lost my father, too."

When Slater fails to respond, Anderson pipes up, "Yeah, I saw that article about your father yesterday. He was a remarkable man. My condolences to you and your mother."

Slater instantly turns on Anderson, his eyes flashing in rage. "Don't *ever* bring up that bastard again."

Holding up his hands in surrender, Anderson leans back. "Woah! I had no idea it was a touchy subject for you."

Slater then turns his sights on me. "Let's talk about your father instead."

I meet his hostile gaze without flinching. "My father was a good man. The best, actually."

"Must be nice…" Slater snarls into his glass, taking another sip of whiskey. "You're lucky he was a nobody. I sure wish my father had been."

Anderson snorts. "Alonzo Davis wasn't a nobody, Surf."

Slater pauses between sips. "Are we talking about that famous violinist who cheated on his wife multiple times before shooting himself in the head?"

I clench my fists, resenting the casual way he defames my father. But I know he's only repeating what the press said about him, based solely on what my mother "leaked" to anonymous sources.

"You have no idea what you are talking about," I reply in a voice far calmer than I feel. "You don't know any more than I do about your father—if I were to believe the press."

Slater grunts, finishing off his drink. "Point taken.

How long has it been since he died?"

"I was fifteen when it happened."

"Huh…that's how old I was when my dad walked out." He sounds surprised when he adds, "I guess we have more in common than I thought."

Slater looks at me, saying in a livid voice, "If it hadn't been for my mother holding down multiple jobs, we never would have survived. My fucking father hired lawyers to make sure he only paid the minimum child support the state allowed."

He then adds in disgust, "All so he could dress his new wife in designer clothes and jet set around the world."

Holding his glass, he toasts, "Thank God for our mothers."

When I fail to lift my glass, he sounds offended. "*What?*"

Meeting his gaze, I state in a voice as cold as ice, "I will never toast to the beast."

Slater's lips curl into a sarcastic smile. "The bastard and the beast. Doesn't that seem like a match made in heaven?"

Before heading down to class the next evening, I stop at the reception desk to confirm that Mistress Blaze will be attending the practicum despite last night's interruption. My enthusiasm for the practicum has not diminished. In fact, my interest has only increased. So, I am relieved when Rachael informs me that the fire play session is still taking place.

The moment I enter the classroom, I sense a tangible difference. With Ashford gone, our classroom dynamic has changed. It's as if an invisible weight has been lifted.

I nod to Slater before taking a seat next to Kat.

She looks amused. "What's going on between you two?"

"We cleared the air last night."

"It's about time he got his act together," Ravenson interjects, pulling out his notebook.

The male submissive from yesterday returns and now stands naked in front of the class. Alana takes up her pointer and picks up where she left off yesterday, continuing the lesson as if nothing ever happened. I stay focused on Alana's words, take detailed notes, and have no problem pointing out the safe and unsafe zones for impact play when she calls on me to stand and name each of them.

But the moment the bell rings, I fly out the door, anxious to begin my first session with fire play. It feels as if I've been waiting forever for this chance.

Padded leather tables are spaced far apart in the large room in a circular pattern with Mistress Blaze as the focal point. It will allow her to watch and respond quickly to each of us.

A jar of fuel, a bucket of water, a fire blanket, water-soaked towels, and an extinguisher have been set out beside each table. I open my tool bag and set out the two fire wands I purchased for tonight.

Master Nosh stands in the room and informs us, "As

you can see, we have prepared you with all of the necessary items needed should anything go wrong. Fire play is as exciting as it is dangerous, and it is not something an inexperienced Dom should ever attempt alone. Not only will Mistress Blaze be watching over you, but we have a staff member assigned to each student. They will be acting as your spotter and they are prepared to jump in to put out any stray flames."

I can feel the tension in the room increasing, which only excites me more. The knowledge that I will be fully supervised throughout, allows me to navigate this scene with confidence.

I take off my jacket and quickly roll up my sleeves, ready to begin.

Before the submissives are called in, Mistress Blaze reminds us, "Never forget that we can cause harm if we are not diligent. Always be mindful where your fuel is—not just the jar of fuel, but any drips or fuel residue left on the skin."

When the submissives enter, their excitement brings an energy to the room that feels similar to the buzzing electricity of a violet wand.

"Submissives, join your partner for the evening," Master Nosh orders.

My heart skips a beat when the submissive with jet black hair approaches me. Her resemblance to my mother is unnerving. However, she is much younger and her eyes sparkle with anticipation—not the malice of the woman who raised me.

Thankfully, the woman's facial features are not as refined as my mother's, and I quickly take note of all of the subtle differences so I can disassociate her from the beast.

Bowing at my feet, she says solemnly, "I am at your service, Sir Davis." Glancing up, she adds with a shy smile, "I specifically requested to scene with you and am deeply honored to be chosen."

She bows her head again.

I look down at the girl, my internal conflict easing. I remind myself that the woman bowing at my feet has no association with my mother other than what I allow. Closing my eyes, I reset my thinking.

"What name would you like me to call you by?"

"Nova," she answers softly, keeping her head bowed low.

I smile, appreciating her pet name because of my interest in astronomy. "That is a beautiful name."

"Thank you, Sir Davis."

"You will call me Sir, tonight," I command, placing my hand on her head. "Stand and serve me."

She stands, a pleasant smile on her face.

Her amenable countenance stirs the protective nature in me. I want her to thoroughly enjoy my first scene with fire play.

Before we begin, I take a hairband out of my pocket and tie up her hair. "This will be a simple scene," I inform her. "There will be no bondage since I am still new at this."

I smile, adding, "Tonight, I'll be concentrating on the sensation aspect of the fire, not the pain. If at any point it feels uncomfortably hot, I want you to call out 'red.'"

"Yes, Sir."

"Undress for me, nova, and remove all jewelry."

"I am not wearing jewelry, Sir," she assures me. Unlike most submissives, she removes her clothing quickly and looks up at me in anticipation. Normally, I enjoy the slow, sensual movements of a submissive baring herself to me.

However, I approve of nova's enthusiasm to begin because it matches my own.

"Lay face down on the table."

I help her climb onto it and then trace my hand lightly over her skin. I can feel her trembling underneath my hand. Her wide smile illustrates her eagerness to begin.

I could not have chosen a more exuberant partner to scene with.

Laying one of the wet towels over her bound hair to protect it, I command, "Do not move."

I pick up the two wands soaking in the fuel and dab the excess off just as Mistress Blaze showed us the night before. I light one and look down at the blank canvas of my submissive's back.

This is it…

Dragging the unlit swab down her back, I leave a trail of fuel. I then tap the flame against it. I feel an indescribable endorphin rush as the fire races up her back. I immediately follow it with the sweep of my hand and feel the fire briefly as I douse the flames.

"How was that?" I ask.

"Spinetingling, Sir."

Intrigued by the process, I repeat it again and again—alcohol, fire, hand. I watch in fascination as the fire blazes down the trails I make, lingering for a second before I sweep it away.

After I have made several passes across her back, I then move down to her ass. I'm mesmerized by the dancing flames and my power to create and extinguish them.

The experience is both sensual and intimate because of the constant physical connection, but the added element of danger takes it to a whole new level.

I trail the swab down the length of her thigh and watch the colorful flames race up her leg. It is enthralling and addictive.

Mistress Blaze stands beside me, nodding her approval. "This element suits you."

"It does!" I agree.

I can't explain it—possibly, it's the thrill caused by the fire play—but I feel an irresistible attraction to Mistress Blaze. In fact, I have a powerful urge to kiss her.

She smiles alluringly, her gaze focused on my lips, before she turns and moves to Kat's table to watch.

Returning my attention to nova, I continue to tease her with fire until Mistress Blaze claps her hands and announces, "End your scenes."

I trail the swab over nova's back one last time in a circular motion and then tap the flame to it, watching the fire follow the path I've drawn. My hand immediately follows, dousing the flames.

I set the wands in the water afterward and begin wiping her pink skin with the wet towels. I let her know how much I've enjoyed the scene, but what I don't share is how disappointed I am that it's over.

It feels like going zero to sixty in a few seconds and then stopping just as quick—it's a jolt to my soul.

Once she is clean, I climb onto the table and lie down beside her. Rather than end tonight's scene with a passionate coupling, I choose to lightly rub her back while asking her questions about her experience until Master Nosh announces it's time for the submissive to leave.

Nova gazes into my eyes and whispers, "I'm so happy."

I am truly grateful she feels that way, and I kiss her on the forehead.

"It was an honor to scene with you, nova."

Sparks

Later that night, as I head out to the parking lot still flying high from the fire play session, Mistress Blaze calls out to me, "Mr. Davis, can I speak with you for a moment?"

"Of course, Mistress Blaze." I walk back to the entrance, looking at her with admiration as I approach. The woman is striking with her stylish dark hair and the streak of reddish-orange running through it. Based on her youthful appearance, I assume she's older than me—but not by much.

She smiles warmly. "You can call me Natalie."

I nod, honored that she wants me to call her by her given name. "My pleasure, Natalie."

"I know it's late, but would you like to join me for dinner?"

My stomach immediately growls and I chuckle. "Apparently, the answer is yes. You may call me Thane, if you like."

She smiles. "Nosh and I carpooled this evening. Do

you mind if we take your car, Thane?"

"Not at all." I gesture for her to follow me.

As we approach Motivation, I mention to her, "My car has seen better years, but she's seeing me through until I have the money to buy my dream car in a couple of years."

"What's your dream car, Thane?"

"A Lotus."

I open the passenger door for her. As she slips into my car, Natalie tells me, "I like a self-made man."

I shut the door, smiling to myself. Already, the night is off to an excellent start. On the drive to the restaurant, I ask her how she became interested in fire play.

"I was only nineteen at the time. My boyfriend dared me to go with him to visit a dungeon. Understand, neither of us had been to one before."

Her amused laughter rings through the vehicle. "It sounded so taboo and dangerous, but let me tell you, we were not prepared."

"What happened?" I asked, now intrigued.

"I don't even know how Jeff got us in. I guess security was laxer in those days?" She chuckles. "We didn't last long. Jeff called it quits the minute he saw a male sub's cock being tortured."

She then adds in a far-off voice, "But I'll never forget seeing fire dancing across someone's skin for the first time…"

Natalie turns and smiles at me. "I was instantly hooked."

"What happened to Jeff?"

"Eh, turns out we weren't compatible and broke up a

few weeks later. Although it didn't work out, I'll always be grateful to Jeff for that night." She lets out a long sigh. "Unfortunately, the club burned down a few years later and now lives solely in my memories."

"That's a shame. I would have enjoyed visiting the place," I tell her as we pull into the parking lot. "I'll drop you off at the entrance and park the car."

She smiles at me. "Such a gentleman."

When I join her inside the restaurant, she informs me, "This is one of my favorite places. It's a hidden gem that not many people know about, which is rare in LA."

The host near the door tilts his head to Natalie. "Your table is ready, Ms. Ayers."

Natalie leans in. "I hope you don't mind, but I asked for a secluded table."

"Not at all. I prefer it," I respond.

The host leads us to a booth in the back. I admire Mistress Blaze's work and am honored to spend time alone with her.

"I'd ask you how you got started in BDSM, but I already know the answer," she informs me.

"How's that?"

"Samantha thinks very highly of you. She speaks about you often."

I sit back in my chair, looking at her with a profound sense of gratitude. "Thank you for taking Samantha under your wing, Natalie."

She gazes into my eyes, her smile growing. "You've supported her when others would not. I admire that about you, Thane."

Hearing Natalie call me by my given name throws

me off a little, but not in a bad way. It makes the interaction between us feel more…intimate.

A waiter walks up to the table to take our order, interrupting the conversation. After he leaves, Natalie continues, "Samantha is an extraordinary individual. Not many people have the strength to own up to a mistake as severe as hers. Even less have the fortitude to make the corrections necessary."

I pick up my glass and take a drink of water. "I agree. Samantha is incredibly strong."

"She's a natural Dominant. I'm sure you saw that when you began working with her."

"I did…" I feel my heart constrict painfully and confess, "I should have left it to the professionals to train her." I look down at the empty plate, unable to look Natalie in the eye. "I'm partially to blame for what happened."

She chuckles lightly. "Samantha warned me you would say that."

I look at her curiously. "Say what?"

"That you would take the blame for something that sits squarely on her shoulders."

I snort. "I not only introduced her to BDSM, but I tried to teach her everything I was learning at the time."

She reaches over to take my hand. "According to Samantha, you always stressed to her that consent was key. You can't be held accountable if the person under your instruction makes a poor choice."

The waiter arrives with our dinner. Natalie squeezes my hand before picking up her napkin. "Let's take a moment to appreciate this good meal."

I enjoy Natalie's easy manner. Despite having years of experience as a Domme, she treats me as if I were her equal.

Midway through the meal, Natalie stops and sets down her fork. "I once had a promising student whom I poured all of my knowledge into. I learned later that he was responsible for sending a submissive to the hospital with third-degree burns. Naturally, I was devastated to hear it." She pauses a moment, looking at me thoughtfully. "However, I knew I had done my due diligence. Taking responsibility for his actions would have been foolhardy on my part."

She picks up her fork again. "Now, when I train others, I share what happened. I use that tragedy to stress how dangerous fire is and how quickly a scene can get out of control. In that way, the pain that submissive suffered is not in vain and can act as a warning to others."

I nod, saying nothing as I continue to eat while I digest her words.

I'm caught off guard when I feel her foot brush up against my leg under the table. I look up to see her gazing at me seductively.

The intense feeling of attraction I experienced during the practicum returns in full force.

"You might find this humorous, Thane. I certainly do…" she states. "I have found that when two Dominants are sexually attracted to each other, vanilla sex can offer a safe release for the couple."

I chuckle. "I've never considered such a thing but can certainly see the benefits."

"What do you say we finish up here and test out that theory?"

My cock immediately hardens in response. "I can think of nothing else I would rather do."

"Good," she says, smiling.

When I raise my hand to signal the waiter for the check, she gently lowers my arm. "I failed to mention it, but my brother is the cook and owner. We can leave whenever we like."

I pull out my wallet and leave a generous tip before I take Natalie's hand and help her out of the booth.

"Where would you like to go?" I ask as I open the car door for her.

"Neutral ground is best."

"We passed by a hotel near here," I suggest.

Her eyes are beguiling when she answers, "Perfect."

Heading to the hotel, I can't help asking her, "Why me when you could have anyone at the Center—hell, anyone in the whole BDSM community?"

She eyes me lustfully. "You are not only a handsome man, Thane Davis, but you have a level of maturity that is rare for someone your age."

I smirk. "We're not that far apart age-wise. Maybe four or five years?"

"I turned thirty this year," she laughs lightly.

"Well, you certainly don't look it."

"Age is meaningless to me," she declares. "The only thing that matters is the connection you feel with a person."

"I agree completely."

Natalie insists on paying for the room, but to protect

our privacy, I make sure to register it under a false name.

Full of bravado leading up to this moment, once I enter the hotel room, I'm suddenly hit with a bout of uncharacteristic shyness. Chuckling, I walk over to her and lightly graze my fingers against her cheek. "I must admit, I'm feeling a little intimidated by vanilla sex."

She laughs as she sits down on the bed and slips off her high heels. "That is the great thing about a BDSM scene. The parameters are set and, as the Dominant, you are in complete control."

"Exactly," I agree, sitting on the other side of the bed to slip off my dress shoes.

While I might be suffering from shyness, my cock certainly is not. After shedding my jacket and shirt, I stand up to finish undressing and catch Natalie's eye.

She glances at the bulge in my dress pants and nods appreciatively. "This should be fun."

Once we're both naked, I lie down beside her and take in her body with my eyes—the fullness of her breasts, the sexy curve of her waist, and the small tattoo of a phoenix on her right hip.

I refrain from making the first move, which is a challenge for me.

"Shall we start with a kiss?" she suggests. "A kiss can tell you a lot about a person."

Natalie moves closer and I slide my hand into the deep nest of curls at the back of her head as our lips connect. Her soft moan ignites my rampant desire and the two of us ravage each other. Our bruising kisses deepen as she runs her fingers through my hair.

The chemistry between us is intense, and the

strangeness of vanilla sex adds an element of the unknown as I navigate it. I suck in my breath when I feel her hand grasp my cock.

"Very nice," she murmurs.

Following her lead, I slip my hand between her legs to feel she's already wet with desire. Rather than plow my cock into her, I take my time with Natalie, exploring her skin with my fingers even as my tongue explores her mouth.

"I really like being on top," she growls in my ear. I shift on the bed, and she climbs onto me, straddling my hips.

Natalie stares down at me, her eyes luminous and wild with excitement. "You are too handsome for your own good, Thane," she murmurs. Lifting herself up, she slowly settles on my hard shaft.

I throw my head back, enjoying the constriction of her wet pussy. Grasping her ass with both hands, I follow her movements as I press my cock deeper into her.

Natalie grinds on my cock, taking her pleasure from it while I focus my attention on her breasts. I love watching them bounce, and I squeeze and tease them in sensual adoration.

She leans forward so I can suck her nipples, adding to the building tension our sexual compatibility is creating.

When I find myself teetering on the edge of losing control, I change things up and pull her to me. Rolling, we change positions and I settle between her legs. Pulling out, I slowly press my cock back into her pussy and watch in satisfaction as she takes all of me.

Kissing her chin which glistened with sweat, I brace myself before I start thrusting.

Natalie wraps her legs around me, arching her back to open herself fully to my deeper thrusts. There are no words as our bodies anticipate and respond to each other's desires.

I quickly find myself on the precipice again, and roar like an animal. Rolling around in the sheets, the two of us lose ourselves in our carnal hunger for each other.

The whole experience is visceral and intense.

The control we have as Dominants plays out as we deny ourselves our respective climaxes to make our orgasms more intense. Instead of a power struggle, we work in harmony, giving fully to each other.

Hot and sweaty, we smile at each other as we reach the pinnacle with no chance of turning back. Screaming in unison, we hold each other tight as we ride the wave of our intense climax together.

My eyes roll back in pleasure when it hits, as my muscles take over and I thrust into her repeatedly as I come. She takes my deep strokes, her cries going up an octave as her pussy coats my cock with her watery come.

We lie there afterward in silence, completely and utterly drained.

"Wow," she murmurs, finally breaking the silence.

"Exactly," I agree, turning my head to gaze at her.

"Who knew vanilla sex could be that intense?" she laughs, her voice hoarse from screaming. Grasping her breasts with both her hands, she arches her back and moans in satisfaction.

I stare at her in admiration, reveling in the afterglow of our sex.

"Let's make this our little secret, Thane. As far as everyone else is concerned, you and I shared a nice meal and went our separate ways."

I nod in agreement, not wanting complications. "It would be best."

Natalie looks down at my cock and sighs, a pleasant smile on her lips. "That's a damn fine cock you have there, Thane.

My low laughter fills the room as I pull Natalie to me and growl in her ear. "Is that your way of saying you're ready for round two?"

Ren Nosaka

E ach night, Alana teaches us a new way of thinking, and an experienced Dominant introduces us to a new technique. I find I'm in my element here, enjoying the challenge of the practicums and the chance to expand my skill set. Being stretched mentally and physically in so many different directions is what I live for.

Up until now, every expert has been several years older than I am. So, it takes me by surprise when I enter the auditorium and see Ren Nosaka, dressed in a black kimono, speaking to the trainers.

Kat gapes at the young man as she and I walk up to the front near the stage and sit down.

When he is finished speaking to them, Nosaka turns and sees me. He smiles and bows his head in recognition before walking up to the stage. I notice he is carrying his tool bag.

Kat leans over and asks excitedly, "Do you know him?"

"I do."

I have to admit, I'm shocked to see someone who is several years my junior acting as the expert for tonight's instruction.

Together as a class, we watch as Nosaka lays out a jute mat and sets several bundles of rope on the floor. I notice that every movement he makes is slow, measured, and fluid.

When Nosaka is done, Master Nosh stands up to introduce him to the class.

"We are honored to have Ren Nosaka join us tonight. Do not let his age fool you into questioning his experience. Ren is a protégé who spent his entire life working under the mentorship of his father, a world-famous *bakushi*—a rope master of Japan."

The Head Trainer looks at Nosaka with reverence. "Tonight, Ren Nosaka will be teaching you the fundamentals of Kinbaku, the erotic art of rope play."

Nosaka smiles, nodding to Master Nosh. "Thank you for this opportunity to share my passion for the Japanese art of erotic bondage."

He turns to address us. "Before I teach you any techniques, let me share a bit of history about Kinbaku. In Japan, during the 1600s, rope was used as both a restraint and a punishment. The Hojojutsu ties were deliberately designed to cause harm to a prisoner."

Nosaka pauses for those among us taking notes. "Kinbaku is based on specific rope patterns derived from those ties, but they have been significantly modified to make them safer for erotic bondage."

He smiles. "Recently, the West has taken an interest

in Kinbaku, and people in the community here commonly use the term 'Shibari' to describe it. Let me explain the difference between the two terms. The word 'Kinbaku' literally translates to 'bind tightly,' and it is a verb describing the act. It implies an exchange between two people. In essence, Kinbaku uses rope to decoratively tie and restrain the body for the sole purpose of erotic pleasure."

I notice out of the corner of my eyes that Kat seems captivated by the lesson.

"The word 'Shibari,' simply means, 'to tie.' It is generally used to describe the study of rope, or to refer to the beauty of a finished tie in a photo."

Nosaka laughs lightly. "I have been in the middle of heated arguments about these two terms, but it is actually quite simple."

He walks across the stage as he explains, "In Japan, we use the terms to describe the intent of the rope. If the Dominant intends to create an erotic connection during the process of binding and unbinding the rope, it is considered Kinbaku."

Turning and walking in the other direction, Nosaka continues, "However, if the rope is being used in an artistic pose, where the emphasis and intent are aesthetically driven to highlight the beauty of a finished tie, then it is considered Shibari."

Standing in the center of the stage once more, he faces us, putting his hands behind his back. "I practice Kinbaku. My intent is always focused on the submissive and her experience during the scene. However, I do enjoy creating ties that will enhance her beauty."

He swoops down to pick up several of the bundles. "As far as rope, I prefer jute." He holds up the bundle of tan rope. "However, for decorative bondage, you can also use cotton, nylon, and silk." He holds the different materials up consecutively. The cotton looks like common rope, something you would find at a hardware store, but the nylon and silk are brighter in color and have a sheen to them.

"Each of these ropes has a different feel and strength, and some are easier to work with than others. Tonight, I will be working exclusively with jute."

He sets the other bundles back in his bag but keeps the jute in his hand. "Because the purpose of Kinbaku is erotic pleasure, the process involves not only learning the ties themselves but knowing the pressure points on the body, as well as being aware of the subtleties of your touch and the power behind your caress as you are binding your partner."

He looks briefly at the jute rope in his hand. "I liken it to playing a complicated piece of music. You not only have to know each note, but you must *feel* the music here." He rubs his chest with his palm. "The timing and intensity of each note are important, just as each tie and slide of the rope is against the submissive's skin."

He sets the jute back on the floor in a reverent manner. "That process extends from the beginning, before you pick up the rope, to the end, when your submissive is free from your bonds and lying safe in your arms."

Nosaka adds with gentle emphasis, "It is a living thing—beautiful and temporary. Every step in the process acts as a vital note to create an erotic symphony for the soul, which is the essence and art of Kinbaku."

I feel a stirring in my spirit, responding to the power behind Ren Nosaka's words.

"Before we begin tonight's lesson, I want you to see what it looks like in action."

Nosaka kneels and lines up his bundles of jute in a precise line. Afterward, he stands up and holds his hand out.

A woman I hadn't noticed before stands up from the back of the auditorium. She is barefoot and dressed in a short, red kimono. His smile grows as she approaches him. Kissing her lightly on the lips, Nosaka helps her to kneel on the jute mat using the same fluid movements as before.

Already, the scene has begun…

I have observed Nosaka's scenes at clubs before, but his bondage is specifically tailored to the individual he's partnered with, so the scenes he creates always have a fresh quality about them.

Nosaka moves behind his submissive and kneels as well. After enfolding the woman in his arms, she lays her head back against him. He soon begins to rock her gently. The moment he begins whispering in her ear, I can sense a change in her countenance. Very soon, they rock together in harmony.

Their connection is intimate and mesmerizing to watch.

The sound of a lone flute suddenly fills the auditorium, and Nosaka picks up the first bundle of jute. "Kiss it," he commands.

She presses her lips against his rope.

Nosaka then begins to unravel the jute slowly. "Raise your arms for me," he orders in a seductive tone.

The submissive slowly lifts her arms, and he reaches around her, placing the rope just above her breasts. He slips it into the loop he's made and begins pulling it through. He does it artfully, the rope acting as an extension of himself as it caresses her skin.

Throughout the scene, I can hear the sound of the rope slapping the floor as he maneuvers the long strand of jute and ties it into intricate knots, binding his submissive in a decorative pattern of rope.

I sense an almost darker sexual undertone when he takes hold of her silk kimono and spreads it open, artfully displaying her breasts bound in rope. She is completely helpless, his willing captive.

Nosaka maintains the sexual tension throughout the scene, kissing and touching her body as he binds her hands behind her back. He then lays her down on the mat to begin working on her feet.

When he is finished, Nosaka lies down on his side, facing her, and stares into her eyes as he runs his hands over her body, tracing the lines of the rope.

Kissing her deeply, he moves one hand between her legs. I hear her muffled moan of pleasure as her body responds. She shudders visibly when she comes.

With the same patience and care he took to bind her, Tono Nosaka begins unraveling the rope. The sound of the ends of the rope hitting the floor in a rhythmic pattern as he unties each knot is hypnotizing.

When he is finished, he helps his submissive to stand. She bows to him first and then to us. The woman's skin is covered in intricate marks left by the rope, creating an art form all its own.

There is no doubt I am in the presence of a true master.

At the end of the night, I seek out Nosaka, wanting to catch up with him and see what he's been up to. "Hey, Nosaka."

He turns and nods in acknowledgment, finishing his conversation with Laird before he walks over to me. "Do you have any questions about tonight's demonstration?"

"None at all. You did a fantastic job, Nosaka. In fact, I'm ashamed to admit how woefully ignorant I was of your level of expertise. The intricacies of the knots and the complicated patterns make Kinbaku a challenging technique to learn."

He laughs. "I assure you, it is easily mastered with time."

I shake my head in disagreement. "The knots, possibly, but the profound connection you have with your submissives is unique to you."

He smiles. "That is the level of connection I seek, and Kinbaku is my preferred method of achieving it."

"Well, my hat's off to you. It is truly an art that demands dedication."

"If you ever wish to learn the intricacies of suspension in rope, I would be happy to mentor you."

I clap him on the shoulder. "That is quite an offer,

Nosaka, and I deeply appreciate it. However, it would require more time than I have right now."

"I understand. However, I still owe you for the camera you gave me. Because of your generous gift, I was not only able to make a living through my photography, but it also helped me establish myself in the BDSM community here in LA."

"I'm seriously glad you got some use out of it, but I said you owed me nothing, and I meant it. You did me a favor by taking it. Otherwise, it would still be sitting in a junk drawer, dusty from disuse."

Nosaka smiles as he opens his tool bag and hands me five bundles of jute. "Please let me offer you this in exchange. I conditioned them myself."

I take his jute, fully aware of the honor of such a gift. "Thank you."

"I hope they bring you years of enjoyment."

I place them in my tool bag. "I'm certain they will."

He smiles at me thoughtfully. "It is good to see you thriving here."

I grin, unable to contain my enthusiasm. "In all honesty, I can't get enough. I want to know it all—all at once."

He chuckles. "Although I enjoy knowing the many intricacies of one vocation, I admire your ambition."

I hold out my hand to him. "I look forward to seeing you again Saturday night at the extended practicum."

He smiles and replies, "I do, too." But, as Nosaka takes my hand to shake it, his smile suddenly fades. Looking puzzled, he mutters, "I know this might sound odd…"

The sudden change in his countenance makes me feel uneasy. "What is it?"

He looks at me apologetically. "I feel strongly that I should tell you this, although it makes absolutely no sense."

I chuckle nervously. "Go ahead, out with it."

Looking me in the eyes, Nosaka tells me in a serious tone, "Do not trust what is familiar."

Tainted Love

As I drive home, I ponder Nosaka's odd statement. Meeting Anderson at his favorite diner in LA for a late-night meal of chicken and waffles, I end up mentioning it to him halfway through the meal.

"That Nosaka kid certainly seems to have a sixth sense," Anderson declares between mouthfuls. "Do you remember the night at the Haven when the three of us were chatting and I got a wild hair up my ass and raced out of the club, suddenly coming up with the campaign that saved my father's ranch?"

I nod in remembrance, chewing slowly as I savor the unique combination of savory and sweet that the simple dish provides.

"Nosaka said something cryptic just like that to me." He stops to remember. "'You must conquer perceived limits you set for yourself.' Darned if those words didn't open my eyes and help me see what had been right in front of my face the entire time."

"I'll keep an open mind, then," I assure Anderson,

wiping the remaining syrup from my lips after I take my final bite.

He muses aloud, "Pretty crazy thinking that someone Nosaka's age is already a respected Kinbaku Master."

"I agree. Nosaka's knowledge of the rope and his ability to connect with his submissives on a profound level is quite extraordinary, regardless of age."

What I don't admit to Anderson is that Nosaka's ability to connect on such an intimate level makes me uneasy for some reason that I can't explain.

Anderson misinterprets my discomfort, and tells me, "Don't worry, buddy. Mark my words, your time is coming." Pulling out a pack of gum from his pocket, he says, "Here, have a piece."

I reach for a stick, grunting in surprise at the unexpected jolt of electricity that races through my fingers the moment I touch it. I instinctively snatch my hand away and hear Anderson burst out in laughter at my expense.

"Gotcha!"

I frown. "Seriously? Are we back in grade school again?"

He laughs even harder. "Shock gum never gets old, does it?"

I stifle my laughter, not wanting him to know I find his childish humor amusing. "Are you ever going to grow up?"

"Nope!" he answers proudly, stuffing the pack of gum back in his pocket.

Thinking back on Nosaka, I ask him, "I wonder if what Ren Nosaka said is somehow connected to Ashford. I mean, I didn't suspect the guy because I thought of him as a friend.

He shrugs. "Possibly. It certainly seems to fit."

Later, after the drive back to my place, and as we head up the elevator to my apartment, I confess, "I'm really glad you stayed, Anderson."

He throws an arm around me. "My pleasure, buddy."

I turn to him, "No, I want you to know how genuinely grateful I am."

Anderson looks at me with those intense green eyes. "Life is hard enough. That's why we need friends. I've got your back—always will." He socks my arm. "Besides, I've been working on my tan while I've been here." He rolls down the waistband of his shorts to reveal he has no tan line.

"You're kidding me." I look up at him, shaking my head. "Please don't tell me you're tanning in the nude here."

He smirks. "Okay, I won't. But that tiny deck you have out there is perfect for it, and your neighbors don't seem to mind."

"Oh, hell…"

He winks at me as the elevator doors open. When a woman standing in the hallway smiles at him coyly, he waves to her.

"In fact, I think they'll miss me," he says under his breath. "You just might have to take over when I'm gone."

Still shaking my head as I enter the apartment, I head straight to bed. I'm almost asleep when I catch the flash of my phone, letting me know I've received a text. Curious, I check to see who it is.

Smiling, I immediately dial the number and lay my head back on my pillow as I listen to the phone ring.

"Hey, *moy droog*. I was wondering if you would call back."

"You're lucky you caught me before I crashed for the night."

"How has it been now that the traitor is gone?"

I grin, "It's been going well, actually. Without Ashford, we've all come together as a unit."

"And Surfer Boy?" he asks with a snort.

"Turns out, he's not half bad. He's just got issues with his parents—like us."

Durov states jokingly, "Some people shouldn't have children."

"Agreed. But, if they hadn't, you and I wouldn't exist. So…there is that."

"Fair enough," he replies with a sad chuckle.

Since I'm now fully awake, I start an animated discussion with Durov, detailing everything I've learned during the week. But, the moment I yawn, he stops me. "You need to sleep, *moy droog*. Goodnight."

I chuckle. "But you were the one who called me."

"*Nyet.* I only texted. I'm not to blame if you took the bait."

I'm shocked when I realize he's hung up on me.

"Fucking sadist…" I grumble, setting the phone on the nightstand.

In a matter of minutes, I fall to sleep. With good friends, a tool bag full of quality rope, and another practicum waiting for me tomorrow, I don't have a care in the world.

The setting sun is shining in my eyes on my drive to the Center the following evening, and I curse myself for forgetting my sunglasses.

I'm grateful when I pull into the parking lot. I've managed to maintain my good mood the entire day and jump out of my car. Reaching for my tool bag, I look over the roof of my car while I grab it, and suddenly freeze.

Goosebumps rise up on my skin when I think I see my mother in the distance, walking toward me.

I swallow hard, reminding myself that it's only the submissive, nova. Scanning the parking lot, I don't see anyone else around. Instead of trying to avoid her, as I did with chastity, I shut my car door and wait, wanting to explain why I can't be seen fraternizing with her.

The setting sun beautifully frames her silhouette like a ring of fire as she approaches. "Look, nova, we need to talk—"

I stop midsentence, my blood running cold the instant I realize it's not her.

"I've been waiting for you, Thane."

A car suddenly pulls up beside me and my mother barks, "Get in, son."

I shake my head in shock, unprepared for this encounter.

"I have something for you in the car. You always said you wanted your father's violin."

I glance in the passenger window and see the violin

case. I'm overwhelmed by the feelings that rush through me the moment I see it. It is the only material possession on Earth that has any value to me.

"Get in now, before I change my mind," she states, sliding into the passenger seat as she picks up the violin.

I glance at the entrance of the school.

If I don't go with her, I'm certain my mother will destroy the only thing that matters to me. The only thing left of my father.

Looking back at the violin clutched in her arms, I already know my answer.

With my stomach in knots, I slip into the back seat, and the car lurches forward. The man driving the vehicle is someone I have never seen before. I make a quick inventory of his face, noting his neck tattoos. But the man never looks in my direction or speaks, keeping his eyes on the road during the entire drive.

My mother turns in the front seat to look back at me. She smiles with those cruel red lips as she pats the violin case in her arms.

I turn my head to stare out the window. I realize now that Nosaka's warning was about my mother.

She is the boa constrictor in my dream, determined to suck the life out of me, but I've realized it too late.

I should have run…

The driver pulls up to the house.

I wasn't prepared to see it again and my anxiety boils

over.

My mother clutches the violin case tightly to her chest as she gets out of the car. Turning to face me, she slowly opens the case.

I suck in a sharp breath when I see my father's beloved violin nestled inside. It is an heirloom that has been passed down for generations, and it is the one thing that still carries his soul.

I slowly get out of the car, drawn to the instrument like a moth to a flame.

The man in the car drives off while I watch my mother open the door to our house and walk inside without glancing back.

I look up at the house I grew up in as I stand on the porch, fighting back a flood of memories.

"Come on, Thane. Don't leave your mother waiting," she calls out.

"You're not my mother," I growl as I reluctantly walk through the doorway.

I experience a chilling sense of déjà vu as I step into the old house, and I stop for a moment once I'm inside.

It is decorated in the same pristine white I remember from childhood, but my mother has filled the house with expensive things, along with giant paintings of herself that hang on the walls.

She heads to Papa's office and disappears inside.

Ice runs through my veins when I glance up the flight of stairs that leads to their bedroom. That is the place I first caught my mother cheating on my father—the same place he died two years later.

I don't want to be here.

My mother peeks her head out of the office and snaps, "Come on, Thane."

Too invested in the violin to stop now, I lower my head and walk quickly into the office.

The violin case sits on a white marble desk.

When I head for it, I hear the door slam behind me. My hackles rise when I notice one of my mother's pretty boys standing guard at the door.

"What is he doing here?" I demand.

Seeing her with another man in this house instantly throws me back in time.

I'm fifteen years old again, standing in my parent's bedroom doorway. My mother is lying naked in the bed with the "boy toy" she's been fucking. At the same time, I watch my father point the gun at them both, and then himself…

In a voice full of pent-up rage, I scream at the man, "Get the fuck out of here!"

"Now, now, Thane. Don't be such a child," my mother scolds.

I clench my fists as I turn back to look at her, wanting to strangle the beast. Then I glance back at the violin, reminding myself of why I'm here.

"Beau is simply here as my insurance policy," she states matter-of-factly about the man at the door. "Now, do you want the violin or not?"

"Give it to me and I'll leave."

She sits down at a small table next to the bookcase and pats the chair next to it. "We need to have a little chat first."

I narrow my eyes as I take a seat. "What about?"

"You remember how you threatened to slit my

throat with a knife?"

I snort in anger, remembering the hellish confrontation we had just before she was sent to jail. "I only offered to give you a knife. I expected you to do the rest."

She looks at me in disappointment. "What a black heart you have, son."

"I inherited that from you."

Bursting out in laughter, she says, "I must admit, I do see a lot of me in you."

I shut my eyes, wanting to deny it even though I know it's true.

"You are just like me," she states proudly. "To the outside world, you're attractive and ambitious. But we both know that deep down there lies a darkness you can't control."

I grit my teeth. "Is that why you destroyed our family?"

"I'm not the one who pulled the trigger."

Her cold answer rips at my heart.

Gripping the armrests of the chair, I fight the urge to wrap my fingers around her throat.

"There's my boy," she says with an impish grin.

Needing to get far from this place as soon as possible, I growl, "What do you want from me?"

"You owe me, Thane."

"For what?"

She pounds the table with her fist. "For sending me to jail, you little shit! I know you set me up—you and that mealy-mouthed blonde you call a friend."

My heart skips a beat, hearing her make a veiled

threat against Samantha.

"What do you want?" I demand again. I need to get out of this place.

"So glad you asked." She smiles as she pulls out a manilla folder. "Your father had an investment I didn't know about. All I need is your signature and you can leave."

"Why would I give you that?"

She glances at the violin case and raises an eyebrow.

I frown. "How much is it worth?"

"Does it even matter?" she asks, then adds in a childish voice, "*Alonzo's precious violin is priceless…*"

I despise her condescending tone. "I hate you."

"Oh, sweetheart…" she laughs disdainfully. "What makes you think I care? Just sign the damn paper and let's be done with this."

I could care less about the money she wants. I know where I am headed, and I am confident that whatever the amount is, I will be making that on a yearly basis in the near future. Still, I don't trust her.

"Give me the violin first."

She sets down the pen and gets up, walking across the floor with the gait of a supermodel. Picking up the violin case, she waltzes back and hands it to me with a dramatic flair.

The moment I touch it, I'm flooded with a rush of cherished memories. Undoing the latches, I open it up and stare down at the instrument. Even the smell of it reminds me of him.

Papa…

Thrusting the pen in my face, she barks, "Sign it."

I slowly close the case, keeping it on my lap as I sign her fucking document. Handing the paper to her, I growl, "Are we done now?"

Looking extremely pleased with herself, she grins. "I hope that violin is worth the quarter of a million you just signed away, baby boy."

I stand up, unwilling to spend another second in the beast's presence.

She glides over to her boy toy. "Mama's bringing home the bacon, just like I promised."

The man grasps her by the waist, planting a kiss on her lips.

I look away, sickened by the sight of them together.

"There's just one thing," she tells me.

"I'm done, here," I announce, heading for the door to leave. As I go to open it, she pulls out a photograph from her purse and hands it to me.

I glance down at the photo and cringe. The picture is of the three of us—my parents and me—taken the same year my father died. My mother and I are smiling in it, but the beast has scratched out my father's face.

"It's a shame you remind me too much of your father," she tells me.

I glance up to see her nod.

I suddenly realize I've been set up when the man jabs me with a needle. It only takes seconds for the drug to start taking effect. Time crawls to a standstill as I stare blankly at my mother.

The last thing I remember is feeling the violin slip from my hands.

Power of Will

loating in a sea of darkness, I call out to my father. "Papa…"

"I'm sorry, son." His voice floods my mind when he says the last words he spoke before he died.

My heart constricts. Those three words have haunted me ever since that day. They speak to the rashness of the violent act itself—and his regret afterward.

Knowing my father died regretting his suicide adds to the pain.

"I'm sorry too, Papa."

I never told him about the affairs my mother was having while he was out providing for his family—a brilliant violinist playing in crowded venues all over the world. My mother insisted that I keep her affairs a secret, making me her accomplice at the young age of thirteen. I have lived with that guilt ever since.

"I love you, son." Papa's warm voice sounds as real to me now as if he was standing beside me.

"I love you, too, Papa."

A tide of sadness washes over me, but there are no tears, only an overwhelming sense of loss.

"I miss you," I tell him. "I miss our times sailing out on the ocean together, our treasure hunts, and your laughter. How I miss your laughter, Papa."

A chill enters my soul when I confess, "But, I'm starting to forget…"

The sadness I feel threatens to swallow me whole. "I'm forgetting the *sound* of your laughter, the details of your face, the way it felt to hug you—"

I realize now why I blindly followed my mother tonight and gave her exactly what she asked for without question. I'm losing my father.

And that violin is my last connection to him.

"How do I go on without you?"

While I get no answer from him, I can feel his presence.

It is real and tangible.

Knowing my father is close fills me with a sense of joy and, in that brief moment, I feel peace.

I wake up with a splitting headache. Opening my eyes, it takes me a moment to orient myself as I sift through the fog in my brain.

Sitting in the dark, slumped against the steering wheel of my car, I sit up but immediately grab my head when it starts to pound.

"What the fuck…?" I mutter as I look around.

I'm in the parking lot at the Training Center. Glancing down at my watch, I realize tonight's session is almost over. Feeling disoriented, I wonder if I'm dreaming.

The violin.

I scan the car, desperate to find it, but I quickly realize it's not here.

My memories from the night come flooding back. Not only did the beast drug me, but she kept the violin.

Of course she did…

I sit back in my seat, disgusted with myself. "You're an idiot, Thane."

Since I'm in no shape to go to class, I take a few moments to gather myself before starting my car and driving home.

When I enter the apartment, Anderson looks away from the television and frowns when he sees me. "What the hell happened to you?"

Herding me to the couch, he grills me with questions until I spill it all.

"We have to call the police," he insists.

"There's no point. My mother did this as payback for her jail time." I look at him wearily. "I guarantee you the police won't find any evidence to convict her. It would simply be my word against hers."

"But she drugged you!"

"Whatever she put in my system was laced with a hallucinogen, I'm sure of it. It's not worth the risk for me to be associated with drug use, especially when it would only undermine anything I say about her."

"You can't know that," Anderson says.

I smile sadly, condemning myself when I confess, "It's what I would do if I were her."

Anderson sighs, now understanding my dilemma.

Shaking his head, he growls. "I can't believe she made you sign away the money and then stole the violin back."

I shrug, feeling incredibly stupid for believing it would end any differently. "I have no one to blame. I knew she was a snake."

"What do you think she will do with the violin now?"

I let out a long, frustrated sigh. "Most likely, the beast will sell it after she burns through this latest chunk of money." I laugh ruefully. "That, or she'll keep it in the hopes that she can dupe me again."

Anderson looks at me with compassion. "What are you going to do now, buddy?"

Feeling like death warmed over, I shut my eyes and groan. "I suppose I'll call Master Nosh in the morning and see if I can convince him to let me continue despite missing class tonight." I snort, opening my eyes again. "Wouldn't it be funny if I get kicked out of the program because of her?"

"No. It would not be funny at all," he answers seriously.

I stand up, muttering, "Well, I feel like crap and can't think straight. I'm headed to bed and will deal with it in the morning."

"Before you go, drink this," Anderson insists, running to the kitchen to get a jug out of the refrigerator. "It's got electrolytes."

I gulp down the slightly salty fruit drink and thank him.

As I lie in the dark, I find myself struggling to fall asleep. I can't stop thinking about my father's violin. Tears roll silently down my cheeks as I mourn the fact that I will never see it—or him—ever again.

To my relief, Master Nosh allows me to attend class the next day but insists on speaking to me at the end of the evening.

I follow him to his office, and he orders me to sit down.

"The trainers and I found your absence last night particularly disturbing, and it's caused us to seriously question your commitment to the program."

"I assure you last night had nothing to do with my commitment to the program."

"Explain."

I shift uncomfortably in my seat. "To be honest, I'm afraid my answer might incriminate and not exonerate me."

"I hear you speaking in judicial terms, but I am not the law, Mr. Davis. I am simply asking for the truth. Whatever you say will remain within the walls of this establishment."

I look at Master Nosh, desperate to tell him what happened last night—I *need* him to believe me—but I am fearful he won't, and my mother will win again.

"I'm waiting," Master Nosh states impatiently.

"You once told me that you must know a person's history to understand their actions."

He nods.

"I want you to understand my history—all of it. Only then will you be able to understand what happened last night."

Without hesitation, he says, "Tell me."

I spent the next hour sharing details about my family and my life growing up. Even details I kept from my therapists after my father's death. There is something timeless and reassuring about Master Nosh's character that inspires me to be open. I have no feeling of being judged and tell him my life story without hesitation or shame, being brutally honest about myself.

Nothing I say seems to surprise him, and I begin to wonder how much he already knows about my past. Once I've shared my background, I feel free to hold nothing back when I tell what happened the night before.

When I am done, I confess to him, "I realize I was a fool to trust my mother, but the woman understands me well enough to know I would do anything to own that piece of my father again."

"I do not judge your decision," he tells me. "However, I am curious about how you plan to move on from it."

I frown, confused by the question. "I plan to move forward—the same as I have been doing all along. I know my path, and I will not stray from it."

He tilts his head. "So, you are not going to seek revenge?"

I shake my head, having already considered it myself. "She and I are equals when it comes to our calculating nature. While I might be able to destroy her, I could only do it by being as ruthless as she is. That is not the future I choose for myself."

He nods. "It is a wise choice, Mr. Davis."

A few more uncomfortable seconds pass.

Eventually, Master Nosh laces his fingers together. "Unfortunately, I must inform you that a student cannot graduate from the Training Center without having taken all of the classes."

His words hit me in the gut, and I feel as if I have been betrayed. Opening myself up to him only to have a door slammed in my face seems unnecessarily cruel.

"Therefore," he continues, "you will come in on Sunday so Laird and I can instruct you on the lessons you missed."

Understanding floods through me, and I immediately hold out my hand to shake his. I'm stunned that two of the trainers are offering their only day off to help me. "Thank you, Master Nosh. I am deeply indebted to both you and Laird."

He shakes my hand firmly. "Every person has burdens they must overcome, Mr. Davis. What defines your character is how you choose to face them." He glances up at the picture of the Cheyenne chief on his wall. "Little Wolf is an inspiration to anyone fighting to stay true to their vision."

I look at the man in the painting. Little Wolf radiates a calm but powerful confidence. "I would like to hear his story, Master Nosh, if you are willing."

He nods. "As you know, I greatly admire Little Wolf. He fought for liberty and justice in the face of betrayal."

Looking back at the painting, he continues, "The US government promised his people good hunting lands when they were relocated to Oklahoma. But when they arrived, the Cheyenne discovered that they had been lied to. There was no game to hunt because the land was crowded with other Native American tribes, and food was scarce for all."

Master Nosh turns to me. "Imagine the hopelessness you would feel on facing that situation."

I shake my head sorrowfully.

"But Little Wolf was unwilling to watch his people starve to death and announced to the government officials that he was taking his people back to their homelands in Montana. Knowing there would be bloodshed, he promised the soldiers that he did not want to fight but that he would if forced to it. He then ordered his own people not to attack first or attack any civilians."

Master Nosh looks at me with defiant pride. "Although the US agency mobilized many troops to apprehend Little Wolf, he made the long trek back with mostly old men, women, and children. Together, they covered over seven hundred miles before winter. Then, after surviving the harsh winter, he led his people safely into Montana."

"That's incredible," I whisper, amazed that he succeeded against such odds.

Master Nosh gazes at the painting again. "Despite

defying the US government, he was highly revered by all because he never wavered from his promises."

He glances at me. "He is the definition of defying the odds."

"He is," I agree, inspired by Little Wolf's sheer power of will.

"Stay true to your vision, never waver from it, and fight only when necessary. That is the lesson he teaches," Master Nosh states in a solemn voice.

I nod, soaking in that wisdom as I gaze at the painting on the wall.

Master Nosh faces me again, his gaze open and honest. "The staff and I believe in you, Mr. Davis. We admired the way you've handled the conflict with Mr. Slater, as well as how you uncovered Mr. Ashford's deception so we could take swift action. Which is why we are willing to work within the rules established by the Training Center to aid in your success."

I sit there overwhelmed. I have no words.

"You are dismissed."

Overcome with emotion, I clear my throat and manage to say, "Thank you."

I leave the Head Trainer's office a different man than when I entered.

The Art of Flogging

The last week of Dominant training is intense. We learn the ins and outs of sensory deprivation, effective roleplay, edge play with blades, and caning. I can only guess what the final night of instruction will be.

Our class has been informed that there will be a one-on-one critique by the panel in preparation for Graduation Day. I can't believe the course is coming to an end. Frankly, I'm not ready for it.

The accelerated pace has allowed us to cover ground in so many different areas of BDSM, and the experts brought in to train us have been outstanding.

However, the course hasn't only been concentrating on techniques and tools. Every step of the way, they have emphasized the dynamic of D/s and the necessity of maintaining a healthy relationship. The trainers expect us to leave this course knowledgeable and confident, as well as preparing us to become contributing members of the BDSM community outside of these walls.

It is with a mixture of sadness and nostalgia that I

listen to Alana teach her final class.

Looking at us fondly, she begins, "Six weeks ago, you joined the Training Center to become an exceptional Dominant. Some of you came with little knowledge or experience, while others…" She glances at me. "…came with some knowledge but only limited experience."

Her smile widens. "Today, I stand here looking at a group of Dominants I am honored to know. I have full confidence in your ability to lead and care for the submissives under your charge. As you move on from here, you will face challenges, but you have the resources and knowledge to navigate them. As with all of our graduates, you will become a respected part of our community here at the Center."

She leans against her desk. "I feel it is appropriate on this last day to go over the fundamentals as you get ready to enter the community as a representative of the Dominant Training Center."

She laughs lightly. "D/s is an interesting dynamic, isn't it? Submissives hunger to please, and Dominants long to be pleased. It seems like a simple exchange, but as you have learned in class and experienced in the practicums over the last six weeks, it is far more complicated. As a Dominant, you must be comfortable with putting your needs and preference ahead of your submissive's, while still making sure their needs are met."

Pushing off the desk, she walks to the whiteboard. "These are some things I want you to remember as you set out on your journey."

She writes on the board, *Be honest about your limits.*

"You need to acknowledge your hard limits. Some of

you may be unaware of them until you are in the midst of a scene. That's okay. Call your safeword. It's important not to cross lines that you will regret later. The strength of a Dom isn't determined by how far you are willing to go, but by how well you know your own limits."

Alana then writes, *Understand your motives.*

"To be an effective Dominant, it's important to dive into your darker side. Recognize any selfish hunger for power and control you carry inside. It's normal to have darker urges. However, it is wrong to allow them to control you. Acknowledging they are there will help prevent you from crossing that line. When consciously explored, your darker needs can be integrated into a scene in a healthy and powerful way."

She then writes, *Be bold in your role as Master.*

"It is important to be a strong leader as a Dominant. You must not only be good at communicating your desires and rules, but consistent in enforcing and correcting your submissive whenever necessary. If you show weak leadership, your submissive may feel the need to test you and they may lose interest.

"I cannot stress how vital this next one is." Alana looks over her shoulder before writing it on the whiteboard, *Be diligent when choosing a submissive.*

"On the first day, we went over questions that are important to ask before your initial scene with a submissive. But, you also need to be aware that some people who engage in BDSM play are not emotionally or mentally fit for it. If you find they are unclear about their boundaries, if they do not communicate well, or seem emotionally unstable, find a more compatible partner. Your submissive should not only meet your physical needs but your emotional needs as well."

She smiles at me when she writes the final one. *It's okay not to be perfect.*

"When you make a mistake—and you will—be forthright and honest. By exploring BDSM with your submissive, you both accept an element of risk. When a mistake occurs, be quick to make corrections and repair any damage done. Due to the intense nature of the power exchange, and the fact that we are human, you are bound to experience uncomfortable or unpleasant moments. As a Dominant, you must own and accept responsibility, but not condemn yourself for it. Think of it as a path to greater growth."

I smirk, knowing her last comment is meant for me. I'll admit it—being a perfectionist at heart, the thought of failure is still like kryptonite to me. However, through taking this course, I've learned how to navigate a scene that's gone badly, and the necessary steps to take afterward.

I have Ashford to thank for that…

Before leaving class, I walk up to Alana to shake her hand. "Thank you for setting the strong foundation I needed."

She shakes my hand firmly. "It has been a pleasure having you in class, Mr. Davis. I've enjoyed your insightful questions." She smiles, adding, "That insight will serve you well in the years to come."

I nod, honored by the compliment. "I hate that class must end, but I will utilize everything you have taught me."

Her eyes sparkle when she replies, "I am certain you will."

For the final practicum, we enter the auditorium for the last time, and I sit down near the front of the stage with my fellow classmates. We are all curious who the final expert will be.

The trainers wait with us in silence.

When the auditorium doors open, we all turn to see Marquis Gray. "I apologize for being late," he states in a formal tone.

As he walks down to the stage, I realize that Marquis radiates an inner confidence similar to what I felt when looking at the portrait of Little Wolf.

Marquis Gray snaps his fingers before reaching the stage. Immediately, a staff member walks up, placing a small silver chest in the center of the stage before bowing his head in respect to Marquis Gray and exiting.

The trainer mounts the stairs and turns to face us with his feet spread shoulder width apart and his hands behind his back.

Maestro Leo stands up and announces, "It is my pleasure to introduce Marquis Gray, a man renowned for his skill with the flogger, as well as being one of the trainers for the Center's Submissive Training Program."

I join the spirited round of applause.

Marquis Gray nods in response. "It is my honor to

join you tonight. Master Nosh shared with me how impressed he has been with your growth and accomplishments in the past six weeks. I encourage you to never stop pushing yourself as a Dominant. With an open mind, there are untold levels of self-discovery and pleasure to be explored."

He stoops down and opens his silver chest, pulling out a large leather flogger to show us. "As Maestro Leo mentioned, I have come to teach you the art of flogging."

Marquis Gray sets it back in the box before calling out, "Celestia, come join me."

From the back of the auditorium, a woman with long, black hair walks onto the stage and bows at Marquis Gray's feet.

Addressing us, he explains, "I use music to enhance my scenes. I want you to watch and note every detail as my scene plays out. Understand that I am purposeful in all my actions. Afterward, I will explain each element of the scene before I teach you how to properly wield this instrument for maximum benefit and effect."

Turning his attention back on his submissive, Marquis Gray places his hand on her head. "You may stand and remove your dress."

She obediently stands up and slips out of the simple black dress, revealing that she's only wearing a white thong underneath. She waits for his next command, her head bowed respectfully.

"Turn," he commands gently, pulling out a white lace ribbon. When her back is to him, he covers her eyes and secures the blindfold.

With slow, decisive movements, he separates her hair into three sections and braids it, placing the braid in front.

"Place your hands behind your head."

After she complies, he binds her wrists with a white satin ribbon, finishing it with an artful bow. He turns her so we have a better angle to watch before he commands her to kneel.

Marquis adjusts her position, pushing her shoulders slightly forward before reaching into his silver chest and pulling out a piece of red lace. Kneeling down on one knee, he works in silence as he caresses her upper back with it just under the shoulder blades. After stimulating her skin, he sets the lace down and reaches back into the chest.

Taking out a black leather glove, Marquis Gray uses it as an instrument, slapping her skin with it. The soft, alluring sound fills the auditorium.

He then lays down the glove and glides his hands over her pinkened back. "Now that you are properly warmed up, we can begin," he murmurs to her.

The moment the sound of Mozart fills the air, I notice the submissive physically relax. I wonder if she associates the music with the stimulation of his flogger and is already anticipating its caress.

Marquis Gray then pulls out the large, multi-tailed flogger from his chest, and swings it in the air for a few moments to warm up his muscles, before he positions himself behind her.

I watch with interest as he pulls back his arm to deliver the first stroke. The thud of the flogger echoes over the music as it makes contact with her skin. She lets out a charming cry.

"Color?" I hear him ask.

"Green, Master."

He offers a rare smile as he lifts his arm once more. "Enjoy, my sweet."

Marquis Gray's movements are graceful as he swings the flogger. The multiple tails make contact with her skin all at once as he lashes her in rhythm with the classical piece.

Adjusting the power and timing of his lashes to match the music, Marquis uses a circular motion in conjunction with the slower, more melodic sections, and then switches to a figure eight when the composition becomes more powerful and intense.

The auditorium is filled with the sound of leather against skin as he lashes her in time with the music, imparting his passion and devotion to his submissive with every stroke of the instrument.

The joyful smile on his submissive's face as she receives his focused attention is awe-inspiring.

I sit there mesmerized by the beauty of their power exchange.

When I return to my apartment, I am surprised to see Anderson's suitcase sitting next to the door.

"You're headed back to Denver, then?" I ask, throwing my keys on the counter.

"I am, buddy. I've been putting out feelers while I've been out here, and one of the companies I've had my eyes on just asked me to come in for an interview."

I walk over to a hug, patting him on the back several times. "That's great news. I have no doubt you are going to ace the interview."

He grins. "I have a good feeling about it." Glancing at the refrigerator, he informs me, "I went ahead and made you a bunch of meals to tide you over. Just heat and eat."

I chuckle. "You didn't need to do that."

He shrugs, "Least I could do."

"When do you head out?"

"First thing in the morning, and I've already scheduled a taxi so there's no need for you to worry about it."

I let out an exaggerated sigh. "Guess my neighbors will just have to get used to not seeing your naked ass every day."

He smacks my arm. "I do have a surprise for you, though."

I narrow my eyes. "What kind of surprise?"

"Wouldn't be a surprise if I told you, now would it?"

I frown. "You know I have no patience for surprises. Just tell me."

He grins like an idiot. "Not on your life, buddy."

"You're an ass."

Anderson immediately turns around, drops his pants, and moons me with his perfectly tanned ass.

I groan loudly. "Tomorrow can't come soon enough…"

Pulling his pants back up, he turns and smacks my

arm again. "Let's finish off the whiskey and celebrate your graduation and my first interview."

I clasp his shoulder. I know how much I've come to depend on him these last few weeks. "I'd really like that."

Although I hate to see Anderson leave, I'm happy he is stepping out on his own. With a business mind like his, there are no limits to what he can achieve.

Graduation Day

I lay my best suit out on the bed, including the vest and my favorite red tie. Today is an important day for me, and I find myself unusually emotional.

I've worked hard for this day, overcoming challenging obstacles, including my own self-doubt and insecurities. I know I should feel proud, but I feel an aching loss instead. I rub my chest, wishing I could wipe the unwanted feeling away.

Today we will meet with the panel for the final time, followed by a short graduation ceremony. Although we were told to invite friends, I saw no need to inconvenience anyone. I didn't do this for the accolades.

This was the chance of a lifetime, and now I'm watching it come to a close...

I hear a knock at the door and a man calls out, "Delivery!"

I frown, knowing I haven't ordered anything. Dressed in nothing but my sweat pants, I go to the door and open it to see a clown holding a balloon.

"Whatever it is, I don't want it," I assure him, certain this is Anderson's surprise.

"Sorry, sir. I'm obligated to sing or I don't get paid."

I am sorely tempted to shut the door but take pity on the guy and grumble, "Fine. Go ahead."

He takes a deep breath before he starts:

"Happy graduation day to you.

"You live like a shrew.

"You look like a peasant…

"And you smell like one, too."

I force a laugh, wondering if this is Durov's idea of a joke. When I start to close the door, he holds out his hand for a tip.

"Really? It wasn't that good."

He shrugs. "Look, man, they don't pay me enough to even buy lunch."

I grumble as I look for my wallet and pull out five bucks. Handing it over, I tell him, "I highly recommend you find another job."

Taking the cash, he holds out the balloon.

"Keep it," I mutter, shutting the door.

Moments later, he knocks at the door again.

Unwilling to be conned out of more money, I refuse to answer it, but the guy won't let up and continues pounding on my door.

I reach my breaking point and yank it open to find Durov standing there, holding the balloon, a grin on his face.

I laugh. "What are you doing here?"

"The cattleman called and told me he was leaving early and needed someone to spoon feed you so that you get enough to eat."

I burst out laughing and smack him on the shoulder, causing the balloon to escape and float up to the ceiling in the hallway. "You *do* know I am capable of feeding myself."

"Not according to the cattleman."

I open the door wider and invite him in.

Durov gives me a bear hug, then says accusingly, "What's this about a graduation I wasn't invited to, *moy droog?*

"It's nothing. Seriously, it's not worth your time to show up."

He shakes his head. "Are you kidding? I feel like a proud papa. My little Thane all grown up and a big, bad Dom now." When he tries to pinch my cheek, I smack his hand away.

"I didn't invite anyone because it's just going to be a five-minute ceremony."

He looks at me thoughtfully. "Moments like these need to be celebrated with a shot of vodka. Don't you agree, comrade?"

"Just one. I've got to drive in a few hours."

Durov heads to my kitchen and starts riffling through my cupboards until he finds the Russian-sized shot glasses and vodka.

My phone vibrates and I pull it out to see a text from Anderson.

Happy Graduation, buddy! Is the Russian keeping you fed?

I smirk as I type.

Vodka being poured even as I type this—pickles soon to follow.

I slip the phone back into my pocket and watch Durov pour a generous amount of vodka into each glass before handing one to me.

Lifting his glass high, he proclaims, "Here's to your future, *moy droog*. May you out-Dom the rest of the peasants."

I chuckle, clinking glasses with him before downing the shot, but I quickly realize we don't have pickles. Heading to the kitchen, I dig through my cupboards for the unopened jar. Cracking it open, I hand it to him first.

Durov nods in approval, grabbing a briny pickle from the jar and taking a big bite. When he tries to pour us another round, I put my hand over my glass. "I'm not going to my final interview drunk, Durov."

He snorts, clearly disappointed. "I will make a Russian out of you yet, *moy droog*."

"Fine. As long as it's not today," reply with a chuckle.

I hear another knock at the door and glance in Durov's direction.

"Go ahead and open it," he urges.

I narrow my eyes. "What did you do?"

He gives me a mischievous grin. "Why not open the door and find out?"

"It better not be another fucking clown…" I warn him.

Opening the door, I see Manya and Panya, the Russian twins, standing in the hallway dressed in fluffy parkas and furry boots. "Happy graduation day, Sir Davis," they chant in unison, unzipping their coats to reveal they are wearing nothing underneath.

The identical twins smile beguilingly at me.

"Come in," I tell them, ushering the two inside as I glance down the hallway. I see one of my neighbors gawking at me with raised eyebrows and a wistful half-grin on his face.

Shutting the door, I help the girls out of their jackets and toss the coats on a nearby chair.

"Manya and Panya have come all the way from Russia to fulfill your every desire, *moy droog!*"

I look at the twins lustfully, remembering our "eventful" flight to Russia in Durov's private jet. "I'm honored, ladies."

They bow their heads, giggling sweetly.

I glance at Durov, inspired by his unexpected gift. "Do you want to join us?"

"*Da*, but start without me, comrade. I'm going to have more vodka while I watch."

I guide the girls to the couch and sit down, patting the cushion, wanting them to join me. The two move in unison as they settle on the couch on either side of me. I cross my arms behind my head and order in a low voice, "Undress me."

The twins kneel down on the floor, and Manya pulls off my sweatpants. Panya then slips off my boxers before the two of them rejoin me on the couch.

The two girls stare at my rigid shaft, licking their lips

excitedly while they wait for my next command.

I turn my head, kissing each of them on the lips before offering them a challenge.

"Take me to the edge, ladies."

The sisters smile as they eagerly descend on my cock. The two work in unison, and I let out a low groan as I feel their two mouths licking and nibbling the length of my cock, while intermittently sucking my balls. Closing my eyes, I give in to the constant but varied stimulation.

I smack their asses hard whenever they get me close to the edge, enjoying the contact of my hand against their skin and the lovely sound it makes as it echoes in my apartment. I have to admit, the twins are exceedingly good at what they do, and it doesn't take long before I'm teetering on the precipice.

I glance over at Durov. "You ready to join the fun?"

"*Da,*" he replies in a husky tone.

"Let's take this to the bedroom, ladies," I tell the twins.

As the four of us head into the room, I realize I've left my suit lying on the bed. "Move my clothes to the living room," I command them. "You will dress me when we are done."

Their eyes light up as they hurry to do my bidding.

Upon their return, I order the twins to lie sideways on the bed, face up, each with her head in line with the other girl's pussy.

I settle between Panya's legs while Durov does the same with Manya. Turning to Durov, I give him a cheeky smile and a challenge. "Let's see who can make their sub come first."

"You're on, comrade."

He dives in, and I hear Manya squeak beside me.

Looking at Panya, I tell her, "You are allowed to come as quickly and as often as you like."

The girls reach out and grasp each other's hands while Durov and I get down to business. Competitive by nature, I don't rush the process and risk possibly over-stimulating my sub's clit. Instead, I take the slow and steady approach, slipping my finger into her pussy to stimulate her G-spot while I lick and tease her swollen clit.

The girls moan and start bucking their hips, desperately clutching each other's hands as we ramp our stimulation up. I can feel Panya starting to tense, and I know I'm getting her close.

Just before she reaches the precipice, Manya clamps Durov's head between her thighs. Tuned into each other, the two girls cry out in unison as they come. I almost lose control when I feel Panya's pussy quivering against my tongue.

Turned on by her climax, and with no clear winner in sight, I suggest a new challenge. Flipping Panya over, I pull her up on her hands and knees and issue a final challenge. "Let's see which of us can make our sub come first while fucking her in the ass."

Durov chuckles. "Prepare to lose, *moy droog.*"

Inspired, I order the twins to face each other and tell Manya, "I want you to see your sister's face when she comes first."

Durov laughs, "It's the other way around, comrade." He slaps Manya's ass playfully. "Isn't that right, Manya?"

"Yes, Rytsar," she purrs.

Grabbing the lubricant from my nightstand, I squeeze some into my hand before tossing it to Durov.

After my cock is thoroughly lubed, I clean off my hands and gaze down at Panya's perfect rosette. Just as I did while eating her, I take my time, penetrating her tight ass with the head of my cock. I groan in sheer pleasure, gripping her buttocks with both hands as I start rocking my hips.

Panya arches her back, moaning with desire as I push my shaft deeper into her. I stroke her slowly at first, letting her body adjust to the sensual invasion.

Then, when I feel she is ready, I grab her hips and thrust even deeper.

I look to see the two girls staring at each other, their mouths open in the shape of perfect O's as they take our challenging strokes.

Unfortunately, watching their tits bounce with every thrust while I listen to their lusty cries proves too much. I know I'm not going to last long after enjoying their expert session of fellatio earlier. Rather than fight it, I growl loudly and tell Panya, "I'm about to come in your ass."

Those words set off a chain reaction.

Panya suddenly stiffens. The moment I feel her inner muscles milking my cock as she orgasms, I join her release, pumping her ass full of my come. Manya immediately screams that she's coming, too, and I hear Durov's lusty roar in answer. In a matter of seconds, we all are climaxing together.

Afterward, I'm left panting as I lie beside Panya.

Pulling her close to me, I kiss her on the cheek and then look at Durov.

I nod to him, grateful for his unexpected gift.

The girls enjoy dressing me for the special event. They take their time as they button every button, help me into the vest, and take extra care with my tie to make sure it's perfect. While they work, Durov tells me about the expansions he's added to the Tatianna Legacy Center.

"We now have people coming in from all over the world every month to attend lectures on the lesser-known dialects we are preserving. They come to add their knowledge and input."

"Tatianna would be proud of your efforts," I tell him.

"When I see her on the other side, *moy droog*, I want her to know I honored her well." I see the intense pain burning in his blue eyes.

"You have, my friend." I reach out to him, knowing he still grieves for Tatianna. I can't imagine loving someone as much as he loved her. "The world is benefitting from the love you shared. She sees it."

He nods, his smile returning. "*Da.*"

The twins slip on my jacket and step away, looking very pleased with their efforts.

I glance in the mirror and smile. "Fine job, ladies."

"It was our pleasure, Sir," they answer in unison.

Durov walks up behind me, slapping me on the back.

"You don't look half bad—for a peasant."

I chuckle and jab him in the ribs.

Miss Dunningham smiles as I head to the elevators and calls out, "Happy Graduation Day, Mr. Davis."

I wave and smile back, before stepping into the elevator. When it stops and the doors open, I'm taken aback. The commons area has been transformed for the evening, and it now features black and gold cloth cascading from the ceiling down to the floor on every wall. A stage has been set up at the back, and there are six round tables elaborately decorated for the ceremony.

This is a far more formal affair than I expected.

Kat calls out to me. I turn and see she's dressed in a black latex dress with a plunging neckline and dark eye makeup that sets off her brown eyes and ruby lips.

"You are looking stunning this evening," I tell her.

She looks at my suit, and lightly grazes her fingers over my red tie, nodding in approval. "You clean up pretty well yourself."

Ravenson joins us. He looks distinguished in his tailored, three-piece herringbone suit. "It seems odd we won't be attending class next week, doesn't it?"

"I agree," I answer, feeling a tinge of melancholy. "I'll miss seeing you both."

"What about me?" Slater asks, strolling up to us. He is wearing dark jeans, a partially unbuttoned shirt, and a leather cuff on one wrist.

I smirk when I answer, "You? Not so much."

He punches me in the arm. "Dick."

I look around. "Where's Lofton?"

"He hasn't shown up yet," Slater says, punching me again.

We all turn when the elevator chimes and watch the doors open. I have no words when Lofton steps out. He's shaved his head and is wearing black leather pants and a vest with no shirt. As he walks up to us, the sound of his heavy boots echoes in the large room.

"Talk about a transformation," Kat states appreciatively.

Despite his dark makeover, Lofton blushes on hearing her compliment.

Slater snorts. "Nice hair."

Lofton runs his hand over his smooth head. "I thought it was time for a change."

"It's a good look for you," I tell him.

He gives me a half smile. "Thanks, Davis."

Master Nosh enters the commons and announces, "Each of you will have a twenty-minute evaluation. While you wait, I suggest you come up with a statement that defines you as a Dominant. You will share it with the guests attending the graduation ceremony."

He turns to Ravenson. "You will be first. Follow me."

We watch in silence as he walks down the hallway with Master Nosh.

"Shit just got real," Slater jokes.

"What does he mean by 'a statement that defines you as a Dominant?'" Lofton asks nervously.

"I'm not sure," I tell him.

Kat answers, "I think he's asking for our mission statement. Like a formal statement of our goals and core values."

"Well, crap…" Slater mutters.

I see the brilliance behind the task. What better way for us to prepare to walk our own paths than to define what our future goals and values are?

I'm lucky in that I am the last one called to join Master Nosh for the evaluation. It's given me time to think. As we walk down the hallway in silence, I wonder what the trainers will have to say.

Master Nosh stops and nods to me before opening the door…

The Calling

I walk into the room to see the trainers sitting behind a long mahogany table on a raised platform. Master Nosh instructs me on where to stand before joining his colleagues.

I take a deep breath, trying to calm my nerves as I look up at the four of them. The formal setting definitely adds weight to this moment.

Master Nosh is the first to speak. "Welcome to your final evaluation, Mr. Davis. Before we begin, is there anything you would like to say?"

I nod, collecting my thoughts before I begin. "I appreciate the time and dedication you have invested in my instruction. I came here solely to learn new skills. To be honest, that was my motivation for taking this course. However, over the last six weeks, I have come to understand myself on a deeper level. I can see how essential that is as a Dominant. How can you properly lead someone if you are not centered and sure of yourself?"

I look up at each of them. "I thank you for that."

Maestro Leo nods in response.

"I also want to thank you for having faith in me even when circumstances did not show me at my best. To be given this opportunity to graduate with my classmates means more than you know."

Laird responds simply, "You belong here."

I suck in my breath, his words having a profound effect.

Master Nosh then informs me, "Each of the trainers will now give their evaluation based on their personal observations."

I put my hands behind my back and prepare myself for the gauntlet.

Maestro Leo begins. "I was disappointed the night you walked out of the program to nurse your pride instead of caring for your submissive."

I nod. Although harsh, his words are fair.

"However, you did redeem yourself in my eyes. The second scene with honey not only showcased your ability to make her feel safe but you also adapted the scene as you went along to ensure she wasn't triggered after the accident from the night before. That impressed me.

"I know honey shared with you that she has been burned by wax before. When she and I talked afterward, honey mentioned that while the other Dominants took responsibility for burning her skin before going on to perform a successful wax scene with her, she has never felt as cared for as she did with you."

He pauses for a moment. "I'm curious. What was your biggest takeaway from that unfortunate incident?"

Even though it hurts me to say it, I don't hesitate to answer. "I could have prevented it from happening. Even though the candles had been switched, I should have tested the heat of the wax before it ever touched her skin. If I had, I would have known and been able to adjust accordingly. In the end, I am to blame for her burns, not Ashford."

Maestro Leo nods thoughtfully.

"Although I cannot change the past, Maestro Leo, I will not make that mistake in the future."

"That is as it should be," he replies. "By the way, Mr. Davis, you still owe the Training Center for the fur throw."

I nod, realizing I've failed to follow up on it. "I will make arrangements to pay for the replacement on Monday."

Laird addresses me next, smiling when he says, "I have kept a close eye on you ever since the first day, Mr. Davis. I was well aware of Mr. Slater's failed attempts to provoke you. You showed extreme restraint. It was quite impressive." He nods when he adds, "The fact that you were able to work it out without intervention speaks to your level of maturity.

"I must also commend you for discovering the truth about Ashford. Your shrewdness helped expose his deception." He looks at the other trainers at the table. "We sincerely thank you for that and will be revising our entrance procedures to more effectively eliminate unsuitable candidates."

He folds his arms and leans forward when he says, "There is one last thing I want to mention. While your classmates each chose particular tools to concentrate on, it seemed as if you could never make up your mind."

"Remember when I told you that I wanted to learn them all, Laird? I was being serious."

He chuckles. "Humor me, Mr. Davis. If you were limited to only one, what would it be?"

I smile because the answer is simple. "I believe in the power of touch. Whether it be with your fingers, the soft petals of a rose, or a strand of pearls, I feel touch is often overlooked as a skill set."

Laird sits back in his seat, grinning. "I like that answer."

I turn to look at Vendari Steele when he speaks. "One thing that stood out for me was your ability to take correction. For someone who is a self-professed perfectionist, you are still humble enough to handle criticism.

I nod, telling him, "My ego isn't so delicate that I can't handle thoughtful criticism."

"I'm not sure you are aware of how rare that is, especially among alphas who are not used to being questioned."

The other trainers chuckle in agreement.

"The fact that you accept criticism and seek to improve from it speaks volumes. Even after Ashford was exposed for his actions against you, you never shifted the blame for the failure of the scene from yourself. Most people would have felt exonerated, but you understood that fault still lie with you."

"It's possible I see things clearer than most."

He frowns thoughtfully. "It's more than that. A Dominant must be humble in order to grow. Do you see yourself as a humble man?"

I feel awkward when I admit, "I can't say that I do."

He squints contemplatively as he stares hard at me. "It's possible that your brutal honesty about yourself inspires a level of humility."

"I can't help being brutally honest with myself," I reply. "But I'm glad to know it serves some purpose."

"Only if you focus on growth and not condemnation," he warns me.

"I promise to remember that, Vendari Steele."

Master Nosh is the last to speak, and the one person here who is fully aware of my past. "You possess a unique passion for the entirety of BDSM—not simply a single skill or technique."

I smile when I tell him, "My friends have often joked that I'm a jack-of-all-trades and a master of none. But my question is this, Master Nosh. If I am committed to learning and practicing each tool, why can't I be proficient at all of them?"

He nods thoughtfully. "If one remains focused and diligent, a person certainly could, given enough time."

"Exactly," I say, feeling vindicated.

He leans forward. "Something we haven't mentioned yet, but I was struck by while watching you during the practicums, is your natural teaching ability."

I'm surprised to hear it because I consciously tried to bury that part of myself after my failure with Samantha. I made the decision then that I was not fit to teach anyone.

"I saw it on numerous occasions while you were practicing with your classmates after the nightly demonstrations," he continues. "You effortlessly guided them by example and through pointed questions without even being aware of it. You read people well, Mr. Davis, and can relate to them on a level they easily understand and respond to."

I still can't believe he picked up on it.

Master Nosh laces his fingers together and looks at me thoughtfully. "Mr. Davis, it is not often that I meet a Master as inexperienced as you."

I look at him questioningly, unsure what he means.

"It's obvious to all of us on the panel that you possess unique qualities. Your astute mind, thirst for knowledge, and innate ability to teach make for a rare combination. Coupled with your strength of character and your need to seek unity rather than dissension, all of these qualities are the mark of a true leader."

I return to the commons feeling shaken after the panel. To receive such high praise is unnerving for me.

My classmates gather around and Ravenson asks, "How did it go?"

I take a moment before answering, "Better than expected."

Kat nods in agreement. "They definitely gave me a lot to think about."

Slater swipes his hair back. "Every fucking thing they said hit home."

"I feel the same," Ravenson replies.

"Well, I'm just ready to graduate!" Lofton cries, rubbing his hands together excitedly.

One of the staff members approaches us. "Please follow me. Your guests are about to arrive."

We are taken to a back room where we are told to wait. The reality that we've crossed the finish line of this rigorous course seems to hit all of us, and we remain silent as we wait, listening as the audience takes their seats.

Vendari Steele walks into the room to give us final instructions. "Master Nosh will announce each of you in turn, starting with Mr. Davis. You will stand beside him and then move to the left when he calls the next name. Once all five of you have been introduced, you will be free to socialize with your guests. Do you have any questions?"

We all shake our heads.

"Very well. Follow me."

As I stand quietly with my classmates, waiting to hear my name called, I scan the large commons. I spy Durov sitting alone at a table while the other tables are packed with people. I chuckle under my breath, feeling sorry for the guy since I failed to invite anyone.

The moment Master Nosh calls my name, Durov shoots up from his seat and starts clapping, shouting proudly, "*Za vas, moy droog!*"

I smile to myself, listening to his cheers echo through the commons, as I make my way to the podium.

Standing next to Master Nosh, I stare straight ahead as he announces to the group, "Sir Thane Davis has completed this course and distinguished himself as a future leader in this community."

Durov cuffs his mouth and shouts, "Of course he has!"

I somehow keep a straight face.

There is a polite round of applause after Durov's outburst.

Master Nosh shakes my hand, then states with pride, "Well done, Sir Davis."

Having him call me by my title makes it feel more official.

In a formal tone, he says, "Sir Davis will now share with you who he is as a Dominant."

I look at everyone in attendance, feeling the weight of this moment, and pause for a second.

"I stand before you, thankful for the lessons I have learned within these walls. I've been active in the BDSM community for several years now, and I thought I knew who I was as a Dominant. I realize now I had no direction."

I look at Durov, the man who introduced me to this world, and nod to him in gratitude.

"As a Dominant, I gain deep satisfaction in bringing a woman pleasure. I will continue exploring the sensual boundaries through BDSM to expand my knowledge. My intent is to meet a woman's needs on a greater level while satisfying my own carnal desires. I have found that BDSM involves the entirety of a person and invites a deeper understanding of oneself on multiple levels. I hope to uncover them all and share what I learn while enjoying the benefits of my research."

There is another round of applause, along with some

laughter, as I step to the side for Kat's name to be called.

Alana hands me a plaque and formally shakes my hand. "It has been an honor to teach you, Sir Davis."

I take the plaque from her and smile. "I won't forget what you taught me, Alana."

After the short ceremony is over, I walk off the stage to join Durov. "I'm glad you came."

"Me, too," he says, looking at the empty table and laughing.

I look at my classmates celebrating with their friends and family and ask Durov, "Do you want to cut out early and start on those shots?"

"Must we leave so soon, comrade?" He smirks, nodding to one of the women at the next table who can't seem to take her eyes off him.

I slap him on the back and get up to say my goodbyes to the trainers. As I approach their table, I'm surprised to see Marquis Gray sitting among them.

I nod respectfully to him before addressing the rest of the group, "My friend and I are going to head out—"

"You can't leave, Sir Davis," Marquis Gray informs me.

I assume he's joking and laugh. "Why not?"

Laird smiles. "This is only the beginning of the celebration."

Feeling the awkwardness of the situation, I nod to them before making my way back to my table. I'm not surprised to see three women have joined Rytsar at the table.

Durov grins up at me. "See, *moy droog?* We are no longer alone. There's no reason to leave."

While we converse, the staff brings plates of food similar to the tapas they served us during our breaks between lessons. I suddenly feel nostalgic again and realize how much I am going to miss this place.

Marquis Gray soon joins our table. "Good evening."

Durov grins and stands up to shake his hand. "It is good to see you again, Marquis Gray."

"I trust you enjoyed your tour of the school a few weeks back?" the trainer replies.

"*Da!* I did." Sitting back down, Durov puts his arms around the two women on either side of him and grins.

While Durov goes back to entertaining the ladies, Marquis engages me in a private conversation.

"The trainers are very impressed with you, Sir Davis."

Feeling self-conscious, I straighten the utensils next to my plate. "They did an exceptional job teaching the course. My success was due to their dedication and sacrifice."

Marquis raises an eyebrow. "You do not take compliments well, do you?"

Durov leans over and interjects, "*Nyet*. He does not."

Marquis stares at Durov with a bemused expression while he watches the Russian rejoin his previous conversation.

Turning his attention back on me, the trainer asks, "Do you remember when you visited the submissive auction with your friends a few years ago?"

"Of course," I reply. "I've never forgotten it."

He nods in Durov's direction. "After the auction was concluded, Rytsar Durov returned downstairs and spoke with Mr. Gallant about you."

I laugh. "What did he say?"

"Apparently, he told Mr. Gallant that he felt you would not only be an excellent candidate for the Dominant Training course but that you should also be a trainer at this school."

I glance at Rytsar, shaking my head at his audacity.

"While your friend may be overly enthusiastic, he was also correct. I knew you would perform well in this environment."

I meet the trainer's intense gaze and feel compelled to tell him, "Taking this course felt like breathing to me, Marquis Gray. As if this was what I was meant for. I don't know any other way to describe it."

He nods, looking at me thoughtfully. "Sir Davis, I want you to consider something."

"Absolutely. What is it?"

I'm not prepared when I hear him say, "I believe you may be what the Submissive Training Center needs in a trainer. I felt that way soon after you and I met."

He inclines his head before continuing. "Naturally, you are still too inexperienced at this point. However, based on everything that the Dominant Trainers have shared with me, you have the characteristics we are looking for. And, you passed the test."

I look at him strangely. "What test?"

"At the Submissive Training Center, it is against the rules for trainers to engage with the students outside of class. It was the reason Master Nosh ordered you not to fraternize with any of the submissives you worked with."

I lean forward, telling him in confidence, "I will be

honest with you, Marquis Gray. Part of the reason BDSM appeals to me is knowing I can have meaningful encounters with a woman without needing to become romantically involved. Because of my past, I have no interest in commitment—of any kind."

"Duly noted."

He stands up to leave. "I suggest you spend the next few years applying everything you've learned from this course. Then, when you feel ready, come back and we will talk."

Stunned by his words, I watch him walk away.

As the guests begin to disperse, the five of us are told to wait for Master Nosh.

Before Durov leaves I pull him close and say excitedly, in a low voice only he can hear, "You and I have something to discuss when I get back tonight!"

He grins at me. "I promise to have many shots lined up for you, *moy droog.*"

After the final guest leaves, Master Nosh, along with the three other trainers, come to collect us.

"The next phase of the graduation festivities is about to begin," Laird tells us with a glint in his eyes.

As a group, Kat, Ravenson, Lofton, Slater, and I follow the four trainers down the corridor. I'm surprised when they lead us to the Submissive side of the Training Center.

Master Nosh stops beside a room with double doors

and turns to address us. He smiles proudly at the five of us. "With great sacrifice comes great rewards."

He opens the doors, and we walk inside as a group.

The room is immense and lined with a wide variety of BDSM furniture. But even more impressive than the furnishings, is the incredible collection of tools that I see hanging on the walls. It is a veritable feast for a Dominant.

Standing in the center of the room is a large group of submissives with their heads bowed. To see so many gathered in one place is an awe-inspiring sight. But, when I start spotting submissives I've worked with in the past—lollipop, chastity, honey, and nova among them— I begin to suspect that *every* submissive involved in our training is represented here tonight.

My suspicions are confirmed when Master Nosh states, "The submissives you trained with wish to celebrate with you. You are free to scene with whomever you want, and you are welcome to use any item on the walls."

He spreads his arms wide. "Tonight is about enjoying the fruits of your labors, Graduates."

While the submissives applaud our accomplishment, my classmates move forward to join them.

I hang back for a moment, feeling a chill of providence as I realize the truth.

Ever since my father's death, I have longed for something to fill the empty space in my soul.

This place…it calls to me like a siren's song. I belong here.

This is my destiny.

I hope you enjoyed ***A Master's Destiny!***

Reviews mean the world to me.

Experience the story in a whole new way!

A Master's Destiny audiobook narrated by Connor Crais

Coming soon

~~~~~~~

COMING UP NEXT—The Russian Unleashed

If you want more of the sexy Russian, you can read his standalone

The Russian Unleashed

Available for FREE in Kindle Unlimited!

Rytsar Durov – Fine vodka with a side of sadism.

~~~~~~~

Or fast forward in time to Sir Thane Davis as Headmaster of the Center!

The Brie Collection (Books 1-3)

Available for FREE in Kindle Unlimited!

Experienced the sexiness of Sir as he trains submissives and finds true love.

COMING NEXT

If you want more of the sexy Russian, you can read his standalone book, *The Russian Unleashed*
Available for FREE in Kindle Unlimited!

Reviews mean the world to me!
I truly appreciate you taking the time to review
A Master's Destiny.

If you could leave a review on both Goodreads and the site where you purchased this book from, I would be so grateful. Sincerely, ~Red

Go forward in time with Sir as Headmaster of the Submissive Training Center with the popular series
The Brie Collection (Books 1-3)
Available for FREE in Kindle Unlimited!

ABOUT THE AUTHOR

Over Two Million readers have enjoyed Red's stories

Red Phoenix – USA Today Bestselling Author
Winner of 8 Readers' Choice Awards

Hey Everyone!

I'm Red Phoenix, an author who also happens to be a submissive in real life. I wrote the Brie's Submission series because I wanted people everywhere to know just how much fun BDSM can be.

There is a huge cast of characters who are part of Brie's journey. The further you read into the story the more you learn about each one. I hope you grow to love Brie and the gang as much as I do.

They've become like family.

When I'm not writing, you can find me online with readers.

I heart my fans! ~Red

To find out more visit my Website

redphoenixauthor.com

Follow Me on BookBub

bookbub.com/authors/red-phoenix

Newsletter: Sign up

redphoenixauthor.com/newsletter-signup

Facebook: AuthorRedPhoenix

Twitter: @redphoenix69

Instagram: RedPhoenixAuthor

I invite you to join my reader Group!

facebook.com/groups/539875076052037

SIGN UP FOR MY NEWSLETTER HERE FOR THE LATEST RED PHOENIX UPDATES

FOLLOW ME ON INSTAGRAM

INSTAGRAM.COM/REDPHOENIXAUTHOR

SALES, GIVEAWAYS, NEW RELEASES, PREORDER LINKS, AND MORE!

SIGN UP HERE

REDPHOENIXAUTHOR.COM/NEWSLETTER-SIGNUP

Red Phoenix is the author of:

Brie's Submission Series:
Teach Me #1
Love Me #2
Catch Me #3
Try Me #4
Protect Me #5
Hold Me #6
Surprise Me #7
Trust Me #8
Claim Me #9
Enchant Me #10
A Cowboy's Heart #11
Breathe with Me #12
Her Russian Knight #13
Under His Protection #14
Her Russian Returns #15
In Sir's Arms #16
Bound by Love #17
Tied to Hope #18
Hope's First Christmas #19
Secrets of the Heart #20
Her Sweet Surrender #21
The Ties That Bind #22
A Heart Unchained #23
Whispered Promises #24
Beneath the Flames #25

***You can also purchase the** AUDIO BOOK **Versions**

Also part of the Submissive Training Center world:

Rise of the Dominates Trilogy
Sir's Rise
Master's Fate
The Russian Reborn

Captain's Duet
Safe Haven
Destined to Dominate

Unleashed Series
The Russian Unleashed #1
The Cowboy's Secret #2
A Master's Destiny #3

Other Books by Red Phoenix

Blissfully Undone
* Available in eBook and paperback

(Snowy Fun—Two people find themselves snowbound in a cabin where hidden love can flourish, taking one couple on a sensual journey into ménage à trois)

His Scottish Pet: Dom of the Ages
* Available in eBook and paperback

Audio Book: *His Scottish Pet: Dom of the Ages*

(Scottish Dom—A sexy Dom escapes to Scotland in the late 1400s. He encounters a waif who has the potential to free him from his tragic curse)

The Only One
* Available in eBook and paperback

(Sexual Adventures—Fate has other plans but he's not letting her go…she is the only one!)

Passion is for Lovers
* Available in eBook and paperback

(Super sexy novelettes—*In 9 Days, 9 Days and Counting, And Then He Saved Me*, and *Play With Me at Noon*)

Varick: The Reckoning
* Available in eBook and paperback

(Savory Vampire—A dark, sexy vampire story. The hero navigates the dangerous world he has been thrust into with lusty passion and a pure heart)

eBooks

Keeper of the Wolf Clan (Keeper of Wolves, #1)

(Sexual Secrets—A virginal werewolf must act as the clan's mysterious Keeper)

The Keeper Finds Her Mate (Keeper of Wolves, #2)

(Second Chances—A young she-wolf must choose between old ties or new beginnings)

The Keeper Unites the Alphas (Keeper of Wolves, #3)

(Serious Consequences—The young she-wolf is captured by the rival clan)

Boxed Set: Keeper of Wolves Series (Books 1-3)

(Surprising Secrets—A secret so shocking it will rock Layla's world. The young she-wolf is put in a position of being able to save her werewolf clan or becoming the reason for its destruction)

Socrates Inspires Cherry to Blossom

(Satisfying Surrender—A mature and curvaceous woman becomes fascinated by an online Dom who has much to teach her)

By the Light of the Scottish Moon

(Saving Love—Two lost souls, the Moon, a werewolf, and a death wish…)

Play With Me at Noon

(Seeking Fulfillment—A desperate wife lives out her fantasies by taking five different men in five days)